A KIDS' GUIDE TO BUILDING FORTS

A KIDS' GUIDE TO BUILDING FORTS
Harbinger House
TUCSON
BY TOM BIRDSEYE • ILLUSTRATIONS BY BILL KLEIN

About the Author

Tom Birdseye is a writer and former teacher who currently lives with his family in Corvallis, Oregon. He is the author of ten children's books and lectures in schools across the United States on how to stimulate early interest in reading and writing.

About the Illustrator

Bill Klein is a boy-turned-architect and visual artist living with his family in Cedar City, Utah, where he designs custom homes and works in watercolors and mixed media sculptures.

HARBINGER HOUSE INC.
Tucson, Arizona

Manufactured in the United States of America
♾ Printed on acid-free, archival quality paper

10 9 8 7 6 5 4 3

Library of Congress Cataloging-in-Publication Data

Birdseye, Tom.
A kid's guide to building forts / by Tom Birdseye : illustrations by Bill Klein.
p. cm.
Summary: Presents a brief history of forts, step-by-step instructions for building indoor and outdoor forts, hints on where to obtain materials, and safety tips.
ISBN 0-943173-69-8 (pbk.) :
1. Playhouses, Children's—Design and construction—Juvenile literature. [1. Fortification. 2. Building 3. Handicraft.]
I. Klein, Bill, 1945- ill. II. Title
TH4967.B56 1993
690′.89—dc20 92-45908

CONTENTS

INTRODUCTION 7
OUTSIDE FORTS 13
THE LEAN-TO FORT 16
THE PILE FORT 18
THE LEAF FORT 19
THE WATTLE WORK FORT 21
LASHING 23
SQUARE LASHING 24
SHEAR LASHING 25
THE THATCHED FORT 26
THE TEPEE FORT 28
THE DOME FORT 30
THE SAND FORT 33
SNOW FORTS 35
THE SNOWBALL FORT 37
THE SNOWTRENCH FORT 38
THE IGLOO FORT 41
INSIDE FORTS 45
THE TABLE FORT 47
THE SPLIT-LEVEL CHAIR FORT 48
THE BE-TWIN FORT 50
THE DESK FORT 51
THE SPACE BOX FORT 52
THE FINISHING TOUCHES 55
THE GRAND FINALE 59

INTRODUCTION

PEOPLE HAVE BUILT FORTS FOR CENTURIES. HISTORICALLY, THEY WERE USED TO PROTECT COMMUNITIES OR EVEN WHOLE KINGDOMS FROM INVADING ARMIES, AND WERE THE SITE OF MANY TERRIBLE SIEGES AND HEROIC LAST STANDS.

IN ENGLAND, THE FORT WAS THE LORD'S OR KING'S CASTLE. BUILT OF STONE, WITH HIGH TURRETS, GREAT HALLS, AND DEEP MOATS CROSSED ONLY BY A DRAWBRIDGE, IT WAS THE MOST IMPORTANT BUILDING IN ANY TOWN. KING ARTHUR AND HIS LEGENDARY KNIGHTS OF THE ROUND TABLE LIVED IN SUCH A FORT.

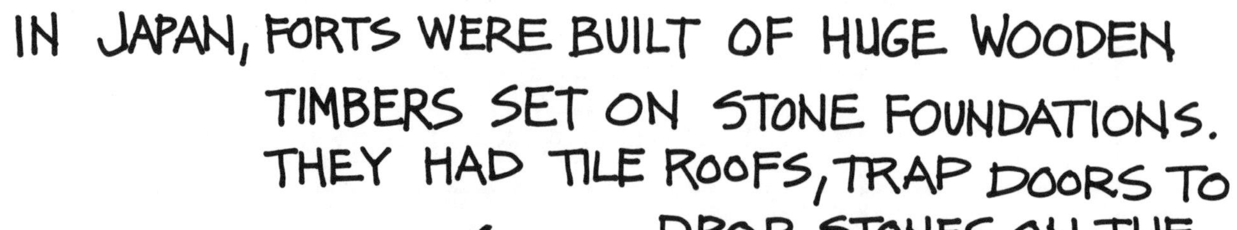

IN JAPAN, FORTS WERE BUILT OF HUGE WOODEN TIMBERS SET ON STONE FOUNDATIONS. THEY HAD TILE ROOFS, TRAP DOORS TO DROP STONES ON THE ENEMY, AND SQUEAKY "NIGHTINGALE" FLOORS THAT ALERTED THE GUARDS IF A NINJA ASSASSIN SNEAKED IN DURING THE NIGHT.

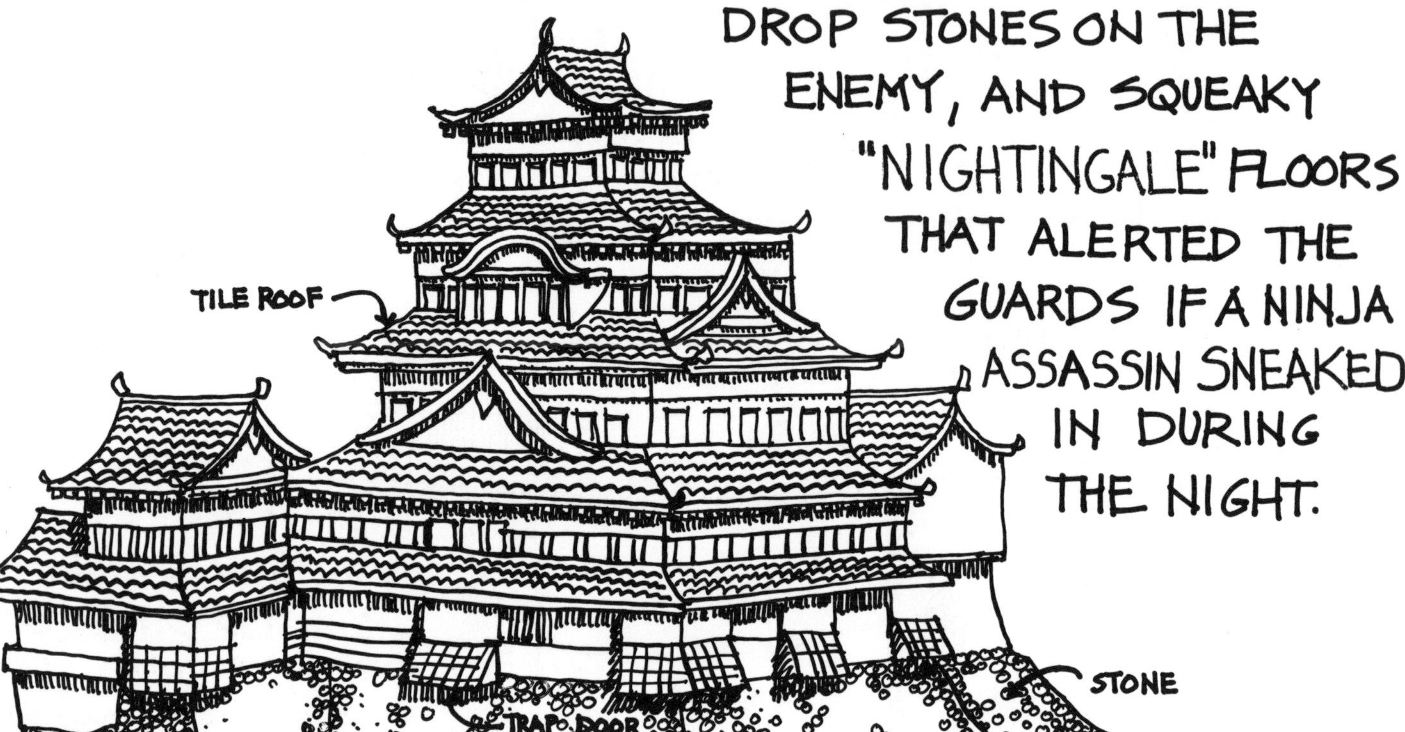

JAPANESE FEUDAL LORDS AND THEIR LOYAL SAMURAI WARRIORS, THE FAMOUS SWORDSMEN OF JAPAN, LIVED IN THESE HUGE, MULTISTORIED FORTS, DEFENDING THEM TO DEATH IF NEED BE.

AND, IN THE UNITED STATES AND CANADA, FORTS WERE MADE OF LOGS STOOD ON END. THERE WERE

HIGH BLOCK HOUSES ON THE CORNERS FROM WHICH TO FIGHT. LIVING QUARTERS INSIDE THE WALLS HOUSED THE CAVALRY SOLDIERS, WHOSE JOB IT WAS TO PROTECT WAGON TRAINS AND PIONEERS FROM ATTACK.

AS YOU CAN SEE, FORTS WERE NOT ALL ALIKE IN DIFFERENT PARTS OF THE WORLD AND AT VARIOUS TIMES IN HISTORY. BUT THEIR MAIN PURPOSE WAS ALWAYS THE SAME: THE SERIOUS BUSINESS OF WAR, WEAPONS, AND FIGHTING FOR SURVIVAL.

THESE DAYS A FORT CAN ALSO BE SOMETHING ELSE, SOMETHING VERY SPECIAL—A HANDMADE, PRIVATE, OFTEN SECRET PLACE FOR KIDS.

IT IS...
A PLACE WHERE YOU CAN SIT, TALK, PRETEND, BE ALONE, MAKE DECISIONS, AND MUCH, MUCH MORE. IT IS A PLACE BUILT BY USING EASY-TO-FIND MATERIALS, A FEW TOOLS, AND SOME IMAGINATION.

IT IS NOT MADE BY DAD OR MOM WITH WOOD FROM THE LUMBER COMPANY. IT IS NOT ORDERED OUT OF A CATALOG AND DELIVERED BY TWO MEN IN A BIG TRUCK. IT IS YOURS, CREATED BY YOU.

AS A CLUBHOUSE, GATHERING SPOT FOR FRIENDS, PLAY AREA, PLACE TO BE ALONE, CAMP OUT SHELTER, OR ANY OTHER OF ITS 1,000 USES, A FORT IS A KID'S PARADISE. OUR WISH FOR YOU IS MANY HOURS OF CREATIVE FUN.

T.B.
B.K.

BEFORE YOU BEGIN

AS WITH MOST THINGS THAT ARE FUN, FORT BUILDING HAS ITS HAZARDS, TOO. THE MATERIALS YOU GATHER MAY HOLD NASTY SURPRISES — SPLINTERS, SHARP EDGES, RUSTY NAILS, AND WEAK BRANCHES THAT SUDDENLY **SNAP!**

THE TOOLS YOU USE (UTILITY KNIVES, HAMMERS, SCISSORS, WEED CUTTERS, ETC.) CAN WORK IN UNPLANNED — **OW!** — WAYS, ALSO.

SO PLAN AHEAD, GET ADVICE OR HELP FROM AN ADULT WHEN NEEDED, AND **THINK** BEFORE YOU BEGIN. **SAFETY** IS THE KEY TO A GOOD TIME. I'LL BE SHOWING UP OCCASIONALLY TO REMIND YOU TO HAVE FUN — A **TON** OF FUN — BUT PLEASE **BE CAREFUL!**

OUTSIDE FORTS
MORE LEAVES!!

OUTSIDE FORTS

THE BACKYARD...
THE VACANT LOT...
AND BEYOND...

OUTSIDE IS USUALLY THE FIRST CHOICE FOR BUILDING A FORT. WHEREVER YOU LIVE THERE ARE LOTS OF MATERIALS TO WORK WITH. CAREFUL SCROUNGING CAN UNCOVER OLD DOORS, WINDOWS, SCRAP PLYWOOD, BOARDS, PLASTIC, OLD CRATES, BOXES, CANS, 2x4's, LEAVES, CLIPPINGS, DEAD BRANCHES FROM TREES, AND A MILLION OTHER USEFUL BUILDING SUPPLIES.

ALL YOU THEN NEED TO ADD IS SOME IMAGINATION AND A GOOD PLAN

SO... READ ON !!!!

THE LEAN-TO FORT

CAREFUL!

TOOLS YOU MAY NEED: HAMMER, NAILS, SAW.

1. FIND SOMETHING TO LEAN YOUR FORT WALL AGAINST. (THAT'S WHY THEY CALL IT A LEAN-TO.)

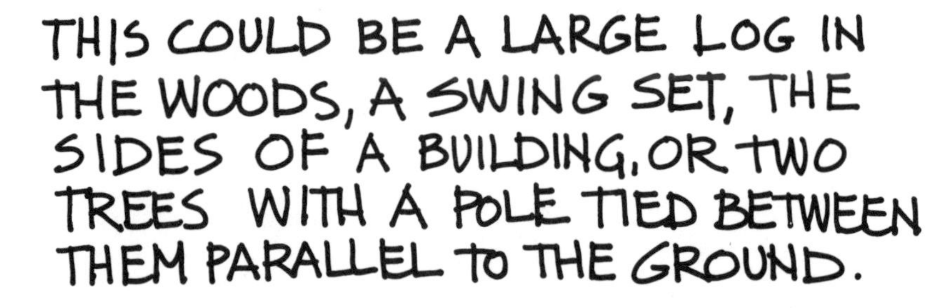

THIS COULD BE A LARGE LOG IN THE WOODS, A SWING SET, THE SIDES OF A BUILDING, OR TWO TREES WITH A POLE TIED BETWEEN THEM PARALLEL TO THE GROUND.

2. LEAN STRONG DEAD LIMBS, DRIFTWOOD FROM THE BEACH, SCRAP LUMBER, OR ANYTHING HANDY AGAINST YOUR SUPPORT AT ABOUT A 60° ANGLE.

CUT THE MATERIAL TO PROPER LENGTH IF NECESSARY. DON'T LEAVE MORE THAN SIX INCHES OF OPEN SPACE BETWEEN THESE PIECES.

60°

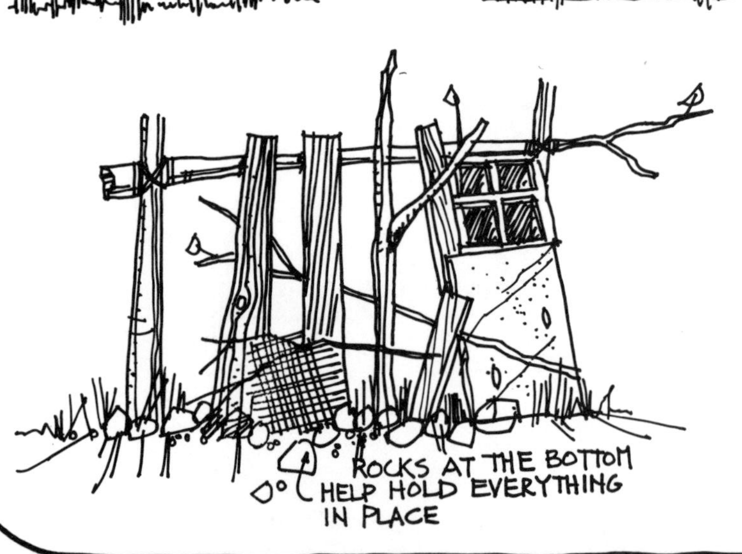

3. STARTING AT THE BOTTOM, AND NAILING WHERE NEEDED, COVER THIS FRAME WITH LEAVES, TREE TRIMMINGS, HAY, JUNK TIN FROM AN OLD ROOF, PLYWOOD, AN OLD WINDOW FOR A SKY-LIGHT, OR EVEN SOD. (SOD

IS A CLUMP OF GRASS WITH THE ROOTS AND SOME DIRT STILL ATTACHED.)
4. PUT THE MATERIAL ON IN LAYERS, LIKE ROOF SHINGLES ON A HOUSE, CAREFULLY COVERING ALL HOLES. THIS WILL RAIN-PROOF YOUR FORT.
YOU NOW HAVE A LEAN-TO FORT READY FOR ACTION!
TOP MATERIAL OVERLAPS BOTTOM MATERIAL
FRUIT
UP
SUU

THE PILE FORT

1. FIND AN EMPTY PACKING BOX BIG ENOUGH FOR YOU TO GET INSIDE. BOXES THAT HAVE HELD STOVES, WASHERS, DRYERS, REFRIGERATORS, OR FREEZERS ARE PERFECT. CHECK WITH YOUR LOCAL APPLIANCE DEALER IF YOU DON'T HAVE A BIG BOX HANDY.

2. TURN THE BOX UPSIDE DOWN OR LAY IT ON ITS SIDE IF IT IS A TALL BOX. WITH A UTILITY KNIFE (CAREFUL-THEY'RE SHARP!) CUT THREE SIDES

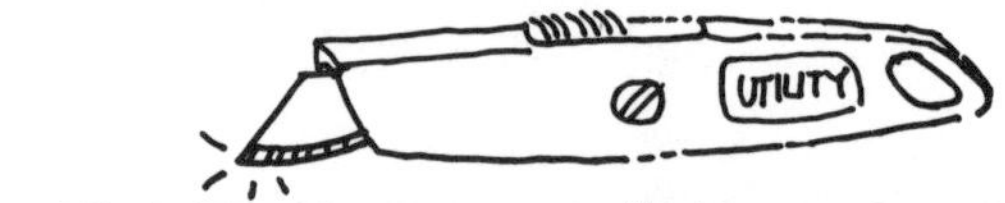

OF A FLAP FOR A WINDOW, LEAVING THE TOP SIDE AS A HINGE.

PROP THIS OPEN WITH A STICK OR TWO. NEXT CUT A DOOR OPENING IN THE SAME MANNER AND PROP THIS OPEN ALSO TO CREATE A FRONT PORCH ROOF.

3. GATHER LEAVES, GRASS CLIPPINGS, HAY, OR WEEDS AND BRUSH.

4. STARTING AT THE BOTTOM, COVER THE ENTIRE BOX — SIDES, TOP, AND ENDS, INCLUDING THE WINDOW AND DOOR FLAPS.

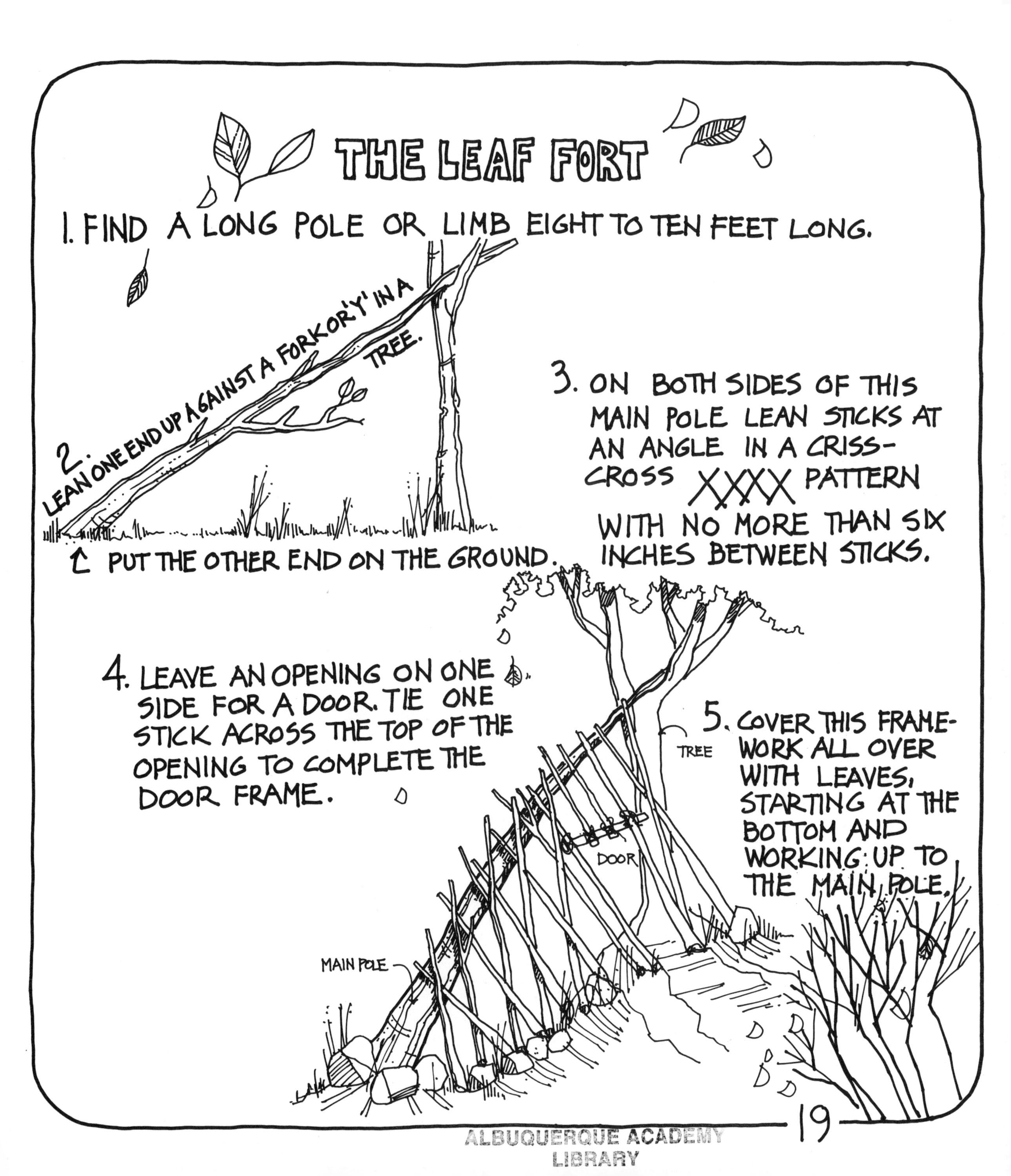
THE LEAF FORT
1. FIND A LONG POLE OR LIMB EIGHT TO TEN FEET LONG.
2. LEAN ONE END UP AGAINST A FORK OR 'Y' IN A TREE.
↑ PUT THE OTHER END ON THE GROUND.
3. ON BOTH SIDES OF THIS MAIN POLE LEAN STICKS AT AN ANGLE IN A CRISS-CROSS XXXX PATTERN WITH NO MORE THAN SIX INCHES BETWEEN STICKS.
4. LEAVE AN OPENING ON ONE SIDE FOR A DOOR. TIE ONE STICK ACROSS THE TOP OF THE OPENING TO COMPLETE THE DOOR FRAME.
5. COVER THIS FRAME-WORK ALL OVER WITH LEAVES, STARTING AT THE BOTTOM AND WORKING UP TO THE MAIN POLE.
TREE
DOOR
MAIN POLE

6. WHEN FINISHED, LAY A FEW STICKS OR BOARDS AGAINST THE LEAVES SO THE WIND WON'T BLOW THEM AWAY.
MORE BRANCHES COMING UP
OK
P.S. IF YOU WANT A REALLY WARM, COZY PLACE FOR COLD WEATHER, PILE ON LEAVES ABOUT TWO FEET THICK. THEN HANG AN OLD BLANKET OVER THE DOOR. LAST, COVER THE FLOOR WITH TWO FEET OF LEAVES. YOU'LL BE AMAZED AT HOW COMFORTABLE THIS FORT CAN BE, EVEN ON A BELOW-FREEZING DAY.

THE WATTLEWORK FORT

1. THIS FORT IS MADE BY STICKING TREE LIMBS ABOUT FOUR FEET LONG TWELVE INCHES INTO THE GROUND. MAKE THE HOLES TO PUT THE STICKS IN BY DRIVING A STAKE INTO THE GROUND AND THEN PULLING IT OUT.

DRIVE STAKE IN TWELVE INCHES AND PULL OUT

HOLE READY TO RECEIVE TREE LIMB

OUTLINE THE WALLS OF YOUR FORT WITH STICK HOLES EVERY TWELVE INCHES, LEAVING A TWO-FOOT SPACE FOR A DOOR. (A WATTLEWORK FORT CAN BE ANY SHAPE YOU WOULD LIKE, PROVIDING IT HAS STRAIGHT WALLS - SUCH AS A SQUARE, RECTANGLE, TRAPEZOID, TRIANGLE ETC.)

- THROW YOUR MOM OR DAD A RINGER. ASK THEM WHAT A TRAPEZOID IS! -

STICKS TWELVE INCHES APART
OUTSIDE ROW
INSIDE ROW
12"
INSIDE OF FORT
2'0"
℄ DOOR

TOP VIEW OF A SQUARE FORT

2. WHEN YOU'VE FINISHED, REPEAT STEP NO. 1, PLACING MORE LIMBS ABOUT TWELVE INCHES OUTSIDE OF THE FIRST SET.

3. NOW, WEAVE THIN BRANCHES IN AND OUT OF THE UPRIGHT STICKS. DO THIS ON THE OUTSIDE ROW AND THEN ON THE INSIDE ROW, NOT BACK AND FORTH BETWEEN THE ROWS. WHEN COMPLETE, YOU WILL HAVE TWO WALLS OF WOVEN LIMBS AND STICKS ALL THE WAY AROUND YOUR FORT (EXCEPT AT THE DOOR) WITH TWELVE INCHES OF SPACE IN BETWEEN.

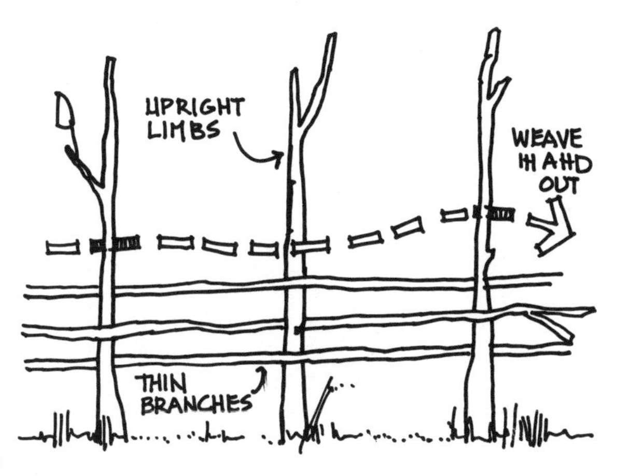

4. NEXT, FILL THE SPACE BETWEEN THE WALLS WITH LEAVES, GRASS, HAY, OR ANYTHING HANDY. THIS MAKES A NICE THICK WALL AND A WARM FORT.

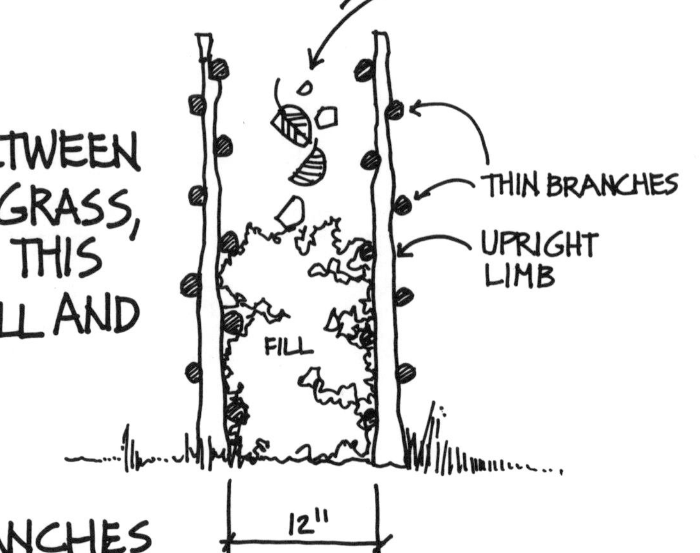

5. FOR THE ROOF, LAY BRANCHES OR LUMBER ACROSS THE TOP, THEN PLASTIC, CARDBOARD, OR TAR PAPER, AND FINALLY MORE BRANCHES TO HOLD THE COVERING DOWN.

6. FOR A FINISHING TOUCH YOU CAN BUILD A DOOR BY WEAVING STICKS TOGETHER WITH GRASS STUCK BETWEEN THEM. AN OLD BLANKET OR RUG ALSO WORKS WELL.

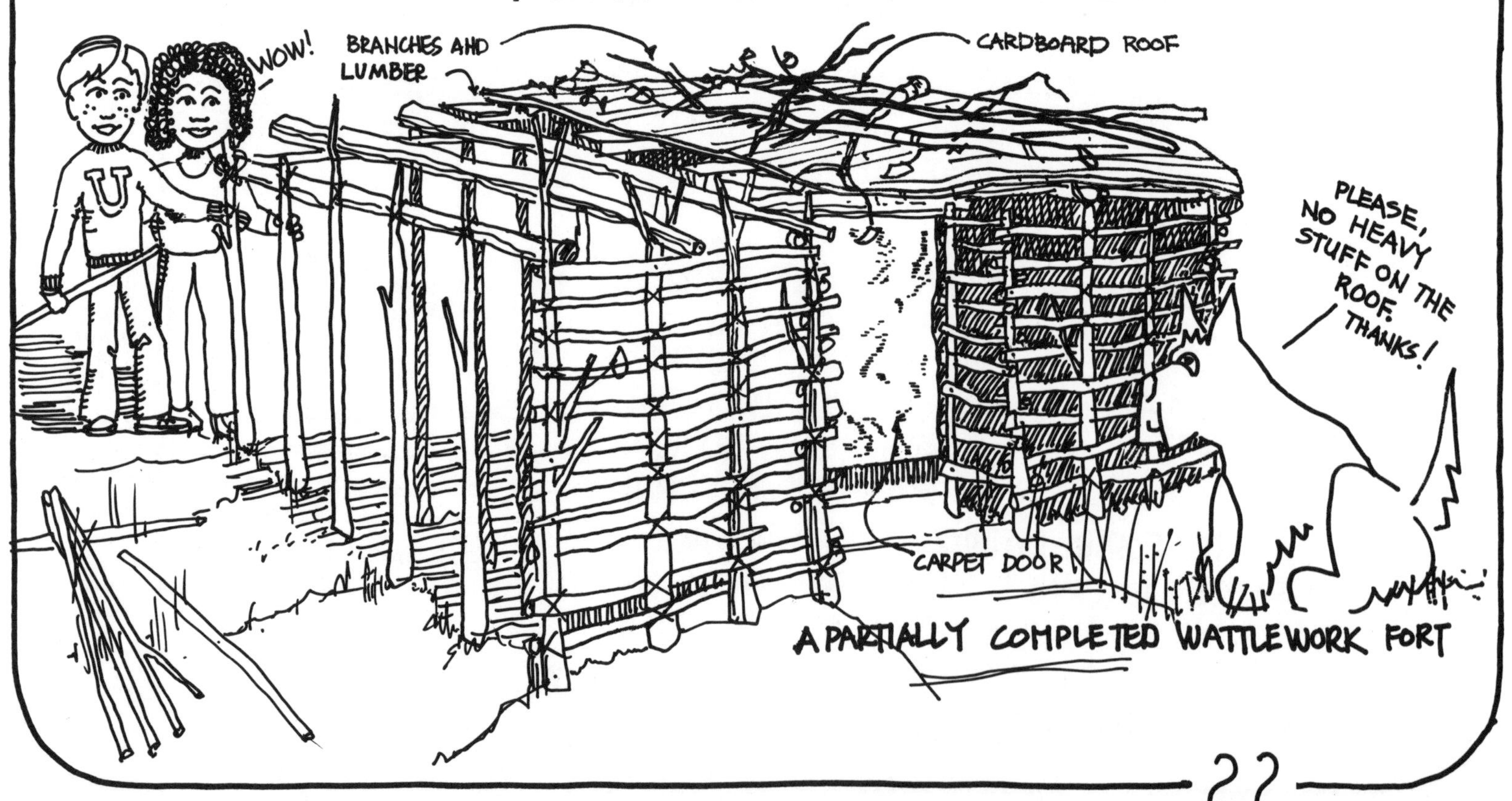

A PARTIALLY COMPLETED WATTLEWORK FORT

LASHING

THE NEXT EIGHT FORT PLANS IN THIS BOOK REQUIRE THAT YOU TIE LIMBS OR POLES TOGETHER IN DIFFERENT WAYS. LASHING IS THE BEST WAY TO DO THIS.

TWO SIMPLE METHODS OF LASHING WILL MEET ALL OF YOUR FORT BUILDING NEEDS: 1. SQUARE LASHING AND 2. SHEAR LASHING

TO BEGIN THESE TYING METHODS YOU NEED TO BE ABLE TO TIE A KNOT CALLED THE CLOVE HITCH.

TO DO THIS:

1. PLACE THE ROPE AROUND THE LIMB AND OVER ITSELF, THEN...
2. AROUND THE LIMB AGAIN AND BACK UNDER ITSELF AS SHOWN.
3. PULL THE ENDS TIGHT. PRACTICE THIS KNOT UNTIL YOU CAN TIE IT QUICKLY AND VERY TIGHT.

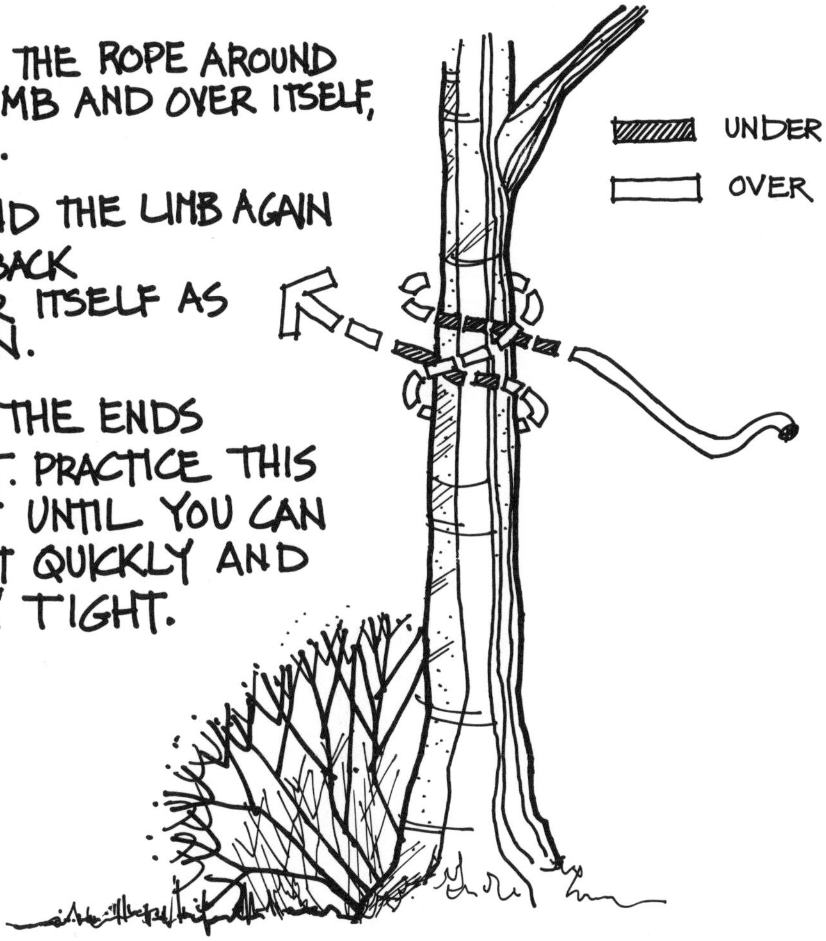

SQUARE LASHING

THIS METHOD OF LASHING IS PERFECT FOR TYING TWO LIMBS OR POLES TOGETHER AT RIGHT ANGLES TO ONE ANOTHER. TO BEGIN:

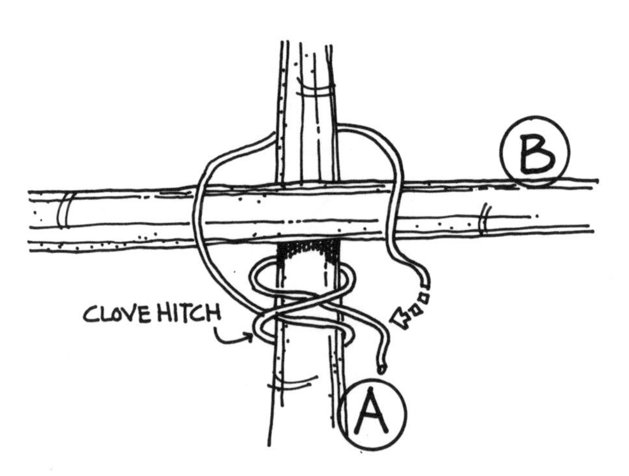

1. TIE A CLOVE HITCH ON POLE (A) SO THAT THE LONG END OF THE ROPE PULLS STRAIGHT OUT FROM THE HITCH.
2. PLACE POLE (B) DIRECTLY ABOVE THE HITCH AT A RIGHT ANGLE TO (A).
3. TAKE THE ROPE UPWARD IN FRONT OF AND OVER POLE (B), PASS IT BEHIND (A), THEN DOWN IN FRONT OF (B), AND BEHIND (A).
4. REPEAT STEP 3 THREE MORE TIMES, THEN TIE IT OFF WITH A CLOVE HITCH.

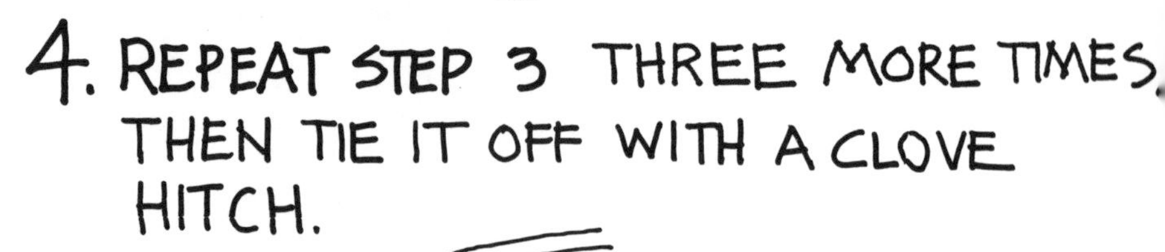

TRICKY!

SHEAR LASHING

THE SECOND METHOD—SHEAR LASHING—IS EXCELLENT FOR BINDING THREE POLES TOGETHER TO FORM A TRIPOD. (A TRIPOD IS A THREE-LEGGED TEPEE TYPE STRUCTURE. "TRI" MEANS THREE. "POD" MEANS FEET. TRI + POD EQUALS THREE FEET.)

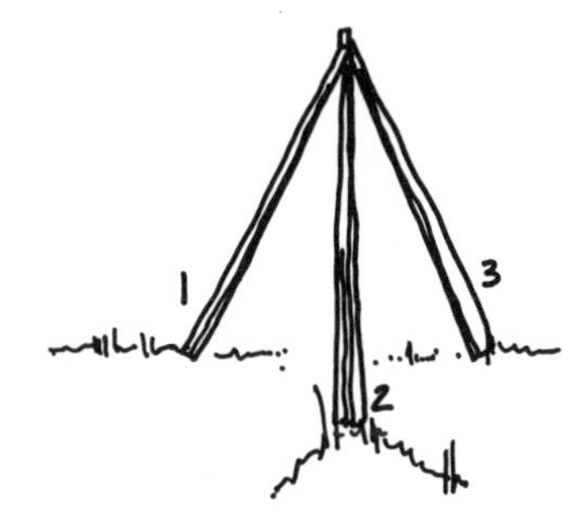

TO BEGIN:

1. LAY THE THREE POLES ON THE GROUND LIKE THIS.

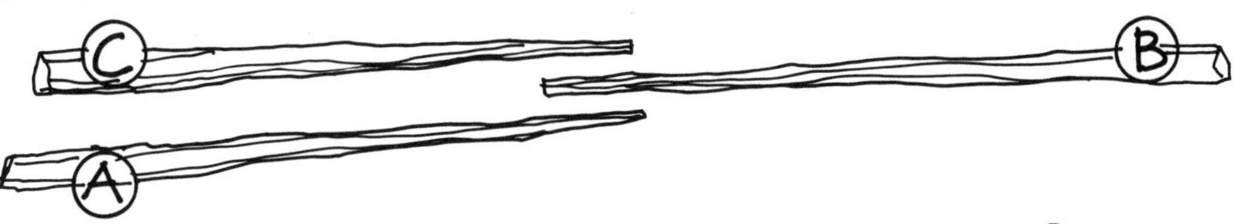

2. TIE A CLOVE HITCH ON POLE (A).
3. MAKE SIX OR SEVEN RATHER LOOSE LASHING TURNS AROUND THE THREE POLES, WEAVING THE ROPE OVER AND UNDER, BACK AND FORTH.

C
B
A
CLOVE HITCH
CLOVE HITCH

4. MAKE TWO OR THREE LOOSE TURNS AROUND THE ROPE BETWEEN (A) AND (B), AND BETWEEN (B) AND (C).

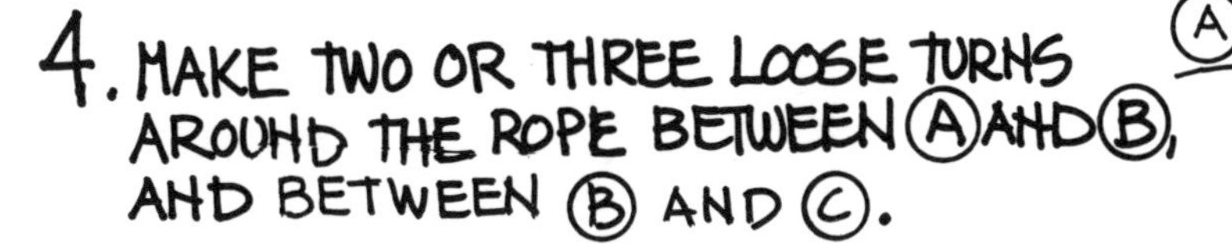

5. END THE LASHING WITH A CLOVE HITCH ON POLE (B). THE TRIPOD IS NOW READY TO STAND UP. IT WILL STAND FIRMLY WHEN THE THREE LEGS ARE SPREAD OUT IN POSITION.

NOW THAT YOU KNOW HOW TO LASH, LET'S CONTINUE WITH THE FORTS.

THE THATCHED FORT

THATCHING IS A BUILDING METHOD THOUSANDS OF YEARS OLD AND STILL IN USE IN SOME PLACES. STRAW IS BUNDLED TO CREATE A THICK, WEATHER-RESISTANT MAT THAT WILL LAST FOR YEARS.

TO BUILD A THATCHED FORT YOU WILL NEED:

- STRING OR TWINE
- POCKET KNIFE OR SCISSORS
- SCYTHE OR WEED CUTTER

1. FIND TWO BRANCHES SIX FEET LONG AND ONE BRANCH TEN FEET LONG. LASH THESE TOGETHER WITH STRING OR TWINE INTO AN OFFSET TRIPOD. USE THE <u>SHEAR</u> LASHING METHOD (p. 25).

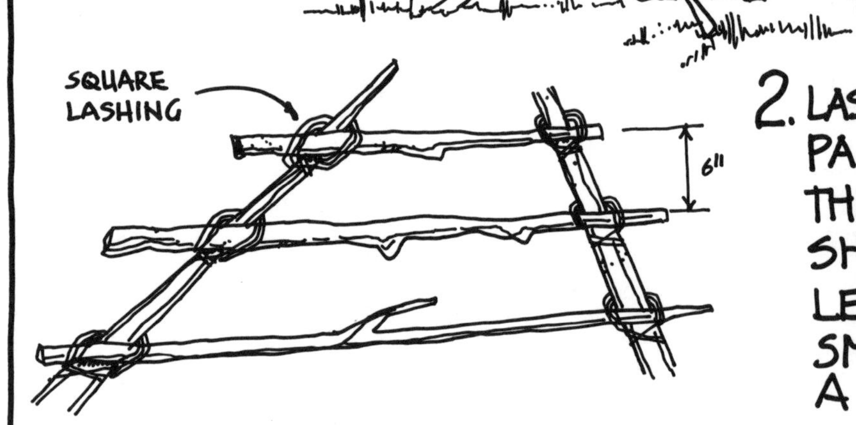

2. LASH LIMBS ON THE TRIPOD FRAME PARALLEL WITH THE GROUND USING THE <u>SQUARE</u> LASHING METHOD. THEY SHOULD BE ABOUT SIX INCHES APART. LEAVE THE BOTTOM HALF OF THE SMALL SIDE OF THE TRIPOD OPEN FOR A DOOR.

3. USING A SCYTHE OR WEED CUTTER, GATHER LARGE HANDFULS OF GRASS OR HAY NO SHORTER THAN FIFTEEN INCHES.

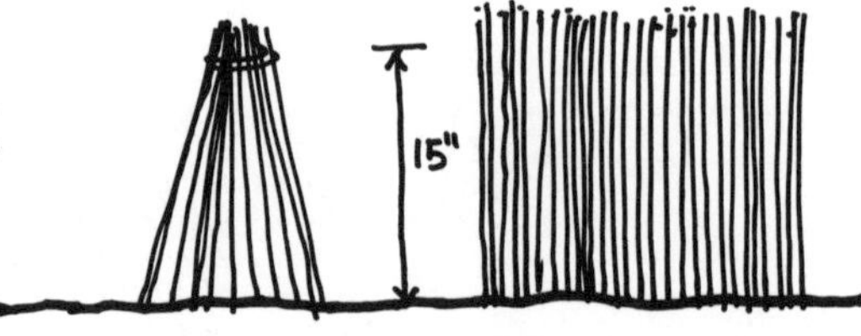

4. BEND EACH HANDFUL INTO A FOLDED BUNDLE AND HANG IT OVER THE HORIZONTAL LIMBS.

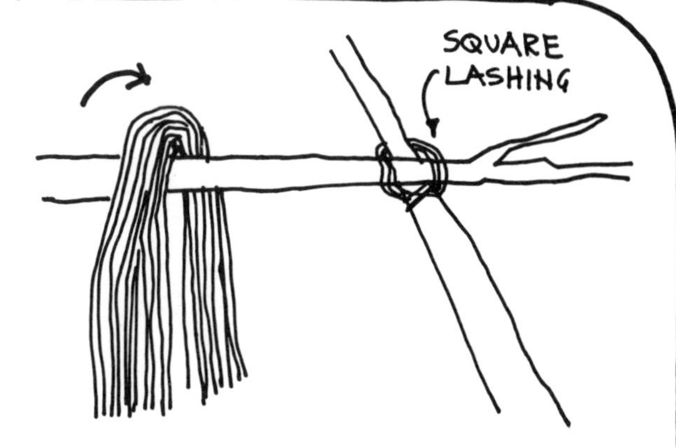

5. TWIST EACH BUNDLE A FULL TURN SO IT WILL STAY PUT.

6. START AT THE BOTTOM OF THE TRIPOD AND WORK UP, OVERLAPPING THE ENDS OF EACH ROW ON TO THE BUNDLES BELOW. BE SURE TO PACK THE BUNDLES IN TIGHTLY SO THE FORT WON'T LEAK. A GOOD TEST FOR THIS OR ANY OTHER FORT IS TO GET INSIDE AND LOOK FOR LITTLE HOLES THAT LET DAYLIGHT THROUGH. IF YOU CAN SEE ANY AT ALL, YOU NEED MORE COVERING MATERIAL.

THE TEPEE FORT

1. CUT TWELVE TEPEE POLES. THESE SHOULD BE TEN

FEET LONG AND TWO TO THREE INCHES THICK AT THE FAT END.

2. LASH THREE OF THEM TOGETHER ABOUT TWELVE INCHES FROM THE SMALL ENDS. USE THE SHEAR LASHING METHOD (p.25).

3. PUT A SMALL STRAIGHT STICK IN THE CENTER OF THE SPOT WHERE YOU ARE GOING TO PUT YOUR TEPEE. TIE A PIECE OF STRING OR TWINE TO THE STICK. MEASURE OUT FOUR FEET AND TIE A SHARP MARKER STICK TO THE OTHER END OF THE STRING.

STICK AT CENTER OF TEPEE
4'0"
STRING
MARKER STICK
MARK OF CIRCLE ON GROUND

4. WALK AROUND THE CENTER STICK, DRAWING A CIRCLE ON THE GROUND WITH THE MARKER STICK. THE CIRCLE WILL BE EIGHT FEET ACROSS. YOU NOW HAVE THE OUTLINE FOR THE BASE OF YOUR TEPEE.

5. STAND THE TRIPOD ON THE CIRCLE WITH AN EQUAL DISTANCE BETWEEN EACH POLE.

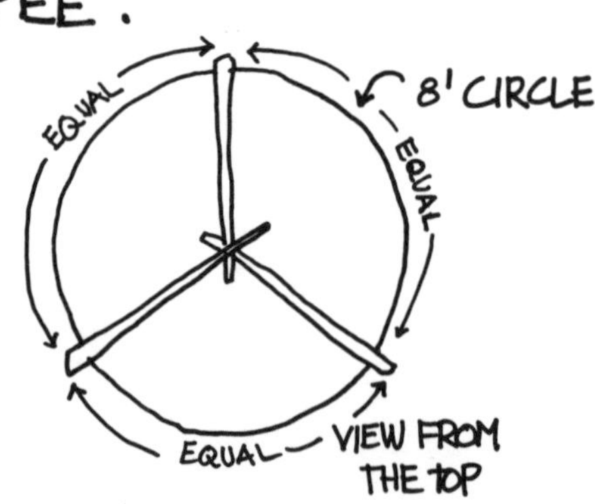

6. LEAN THE OTHER POLES AGAINST THE TRIPOD, PLACE THEIR TOP ENDS IN THE V ABOVE THE LASHING, AND PLACE THEIR BOTTOM ENDS EQUALLY SPACED AROUND THE CIRCLE. A VIEW FROM THE TOP WILL NOW LOOK LIKE THIS.

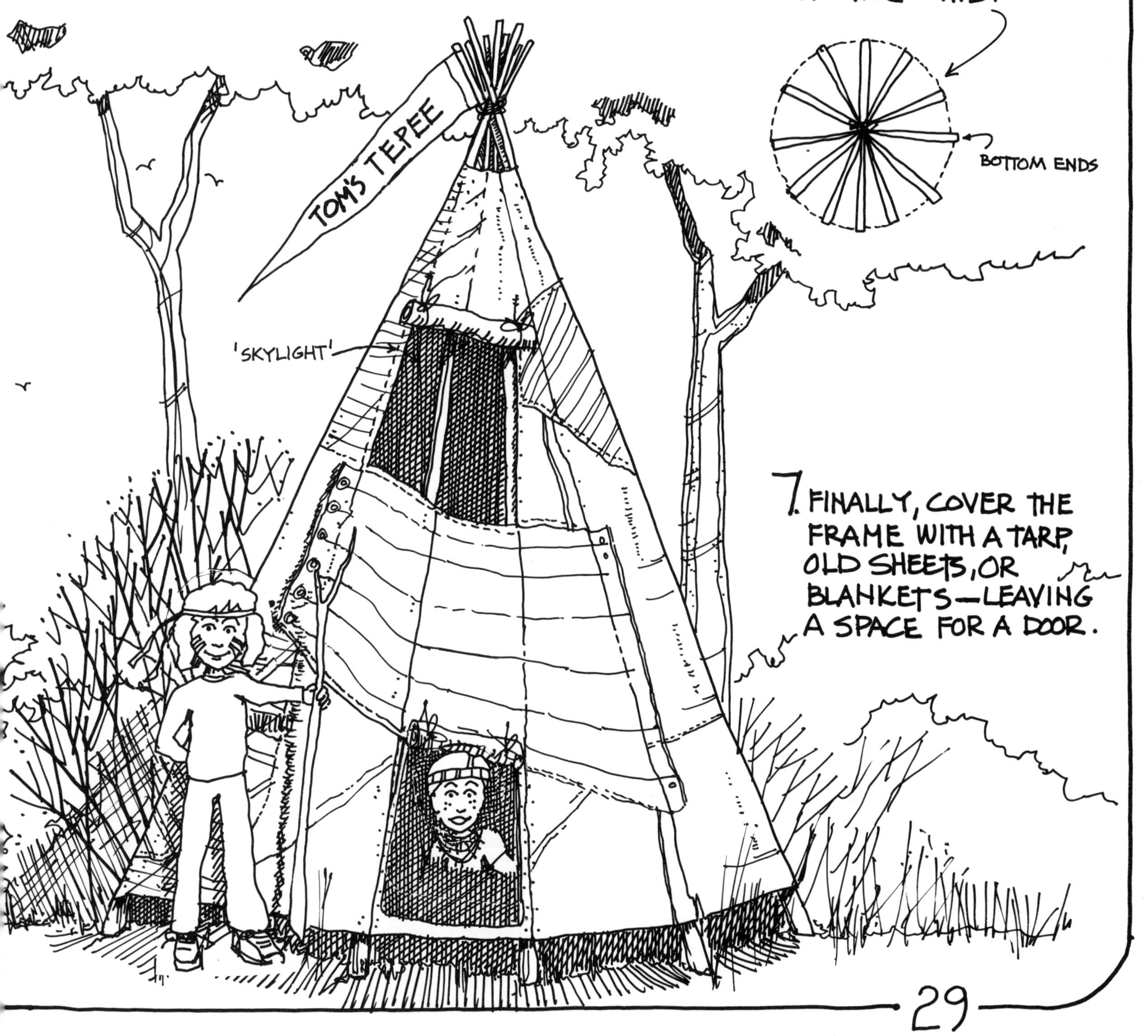

7. FINALLY, COVER THE FRAME WITH A TARP, OLD SHEETS, OR BLANKETS—LEAVING A SPACE FOR A DOOR.

THE DOME FORT

LIKE THE TEPEE, THIS TYPE OF SHELTER WAS BUILT BY NATIVE AMERICANS. COVERED WITH BUFFALO HIDES, IT SERVED AS A SWEAT LODGE.

RED HOT ROCKS WERE PLACED IN A HOLE IN THE MIDDLE OF THE FLOOR. WATER WAS POURED OVER THEM, CREATING A STEAM CLOUD. THIS WAS REPEATED UNTIL IT WAS VERY HOT INSIDE THE DOME. FOR NATIVE AMERICANS, USING THE SWEAT LODGE WAS, AND STILL IS TODAY, A RELIGIOUS CEREMONY PREPARING THEM FOR AN IMPORTANT EVENT.

NO "SWEAT" TO THINK "FORT"!

YOU **SHOULD NOT** USE A DOME FORT FOR A SWEAT LODGE. (IT CAN BE VERY DANGEROUS.) BUT, FOR REGULAR FORT ACTIVITIES IT'S GREAT.

1. TO START, MARK AN EIGHT-FOOT CIRCLE ON THE GROUND. (SEE TEPEE FORT FOR INSTRUCTIONS p.28)

2. PUT HOLES IN THE GROUND TWO FEET APART ALONG THE CIRCLE EDGE.

   MAKE THE HOLES ABOUT TWELVE INCHES DEEP BY DRIVING A STAKE INTO THE GROUND AND THEN PULLING IT OUT. [THE SAME AS FOR A WATTLE-WORK FORT (p.21)].

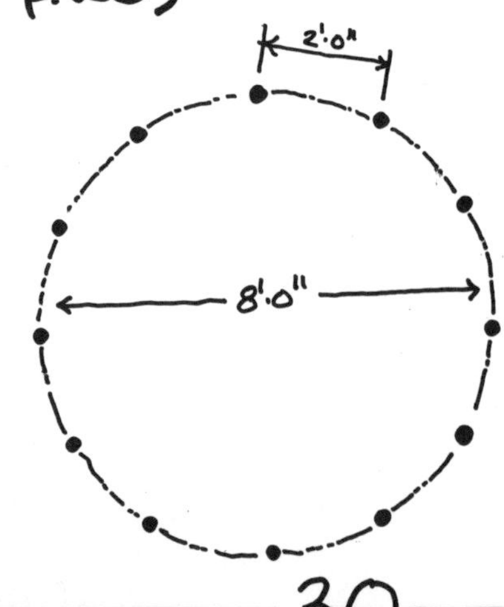

3. GATHER THIN LIMBS EIGHT TO TEN FEET LONG, ONE FOR EACH HOLE.

4. INSERT THE FAT ENDS OF THE LIMBS INTO THE HOLES.

5. TAKE TWO OF THE LIMBS DIRECTLY ACROSS THE CIRCLE FROM ONE ANOTHER AND BEND THEM OVER TO MEET IN THE MIDDLE. THIS WILL MAKE AN ARCH ABOUT FOUR FEET TALL.

LASH THEM TOGETHER WITH STRONG STRING OR TWINE

4'0"

8'0"

6. CONTINUE TO BEND OVER THE OPPOSITE LIMBS, LASHING THEM TOGETHER, AND CROSSING EACH OTHER AT THE TOP, FORMING A DOME.

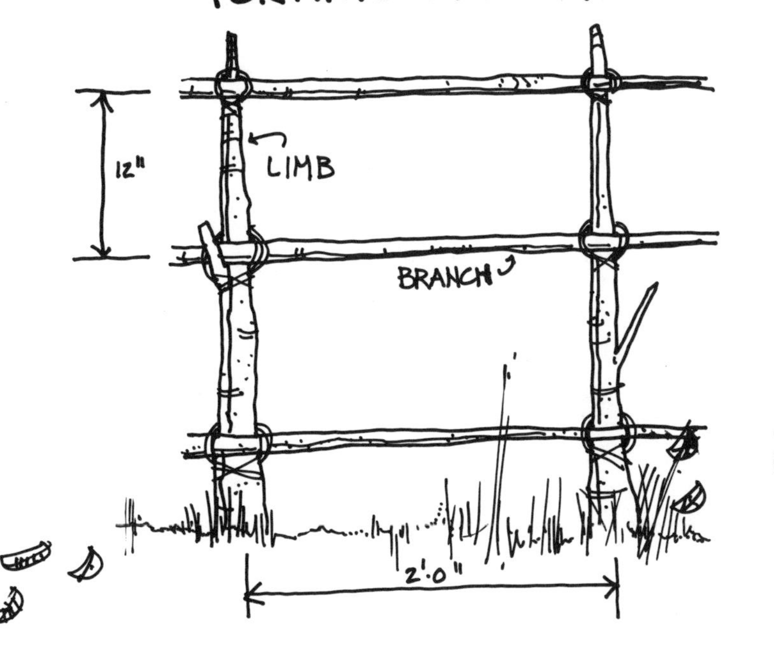

7. NEXT, LASH BRANCHES AROUND THE DOME, PARALLEL TO THE GROUND, ABOUT TWELVE INCHES APART. LEAVE ROOM FOR A SMALL DOORWAY.

THE FRAME OF THE DOME IS NOW FINISHED.

8. COVERING THE DOME CAN BE DONE WITH A VARIETY OF MATERIALS: BLANKETS, PLASTIC, HAY, LEAVES, GRASS, CARDBOARD, OR ANY COMBINATION OF THESE.

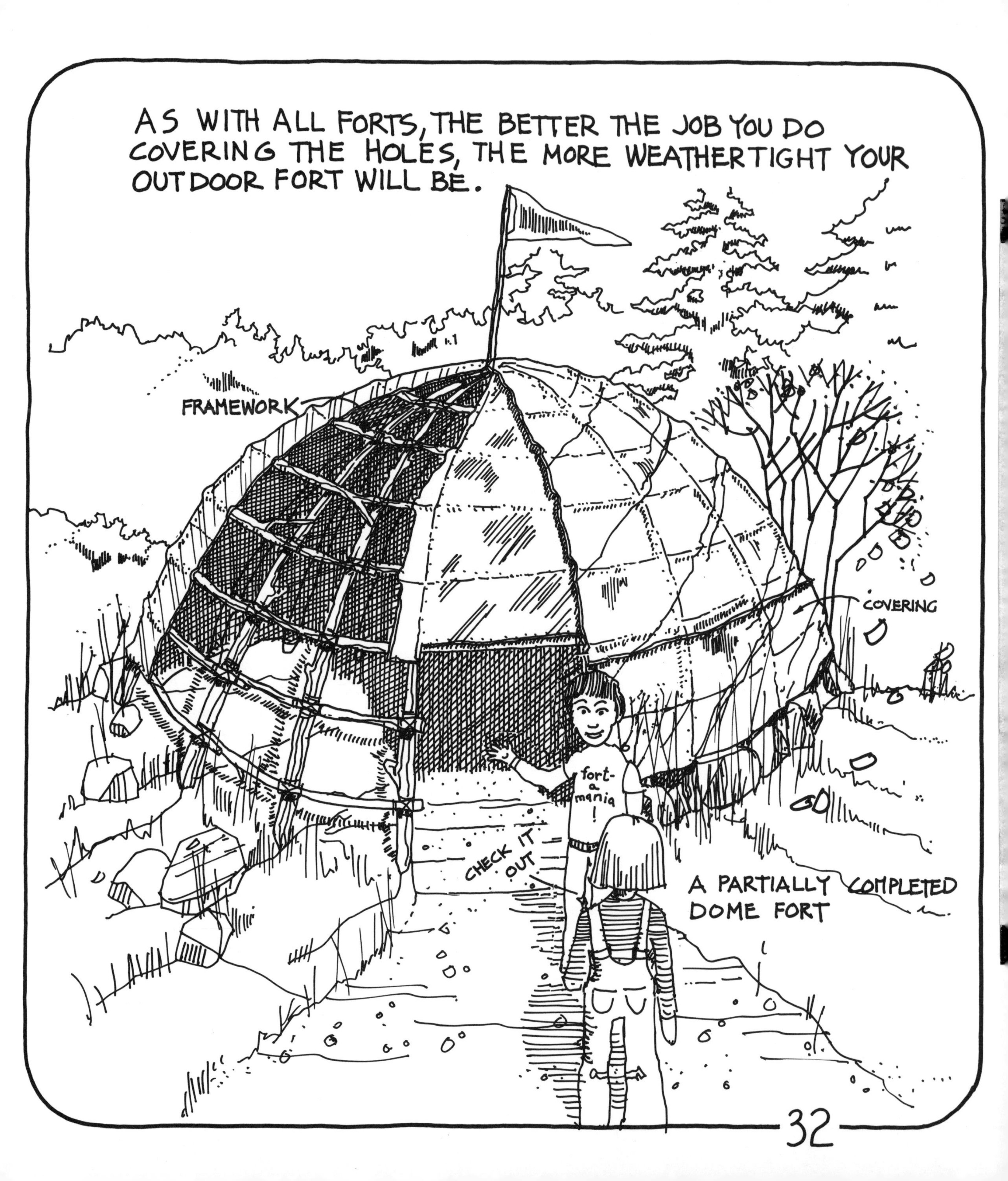
AS WITH ALL FORTS, THE BETTER THE JOB YOU DO COVERING THE HOLES, THE MORE WEATHERTIGHT YOUR OUTDOOR FORT WILL BE.
FRAMEWORK
COVERING
fort-a-mania!
CHECK IT OUT
A PARTIALLY COMPLETED DOME FORT

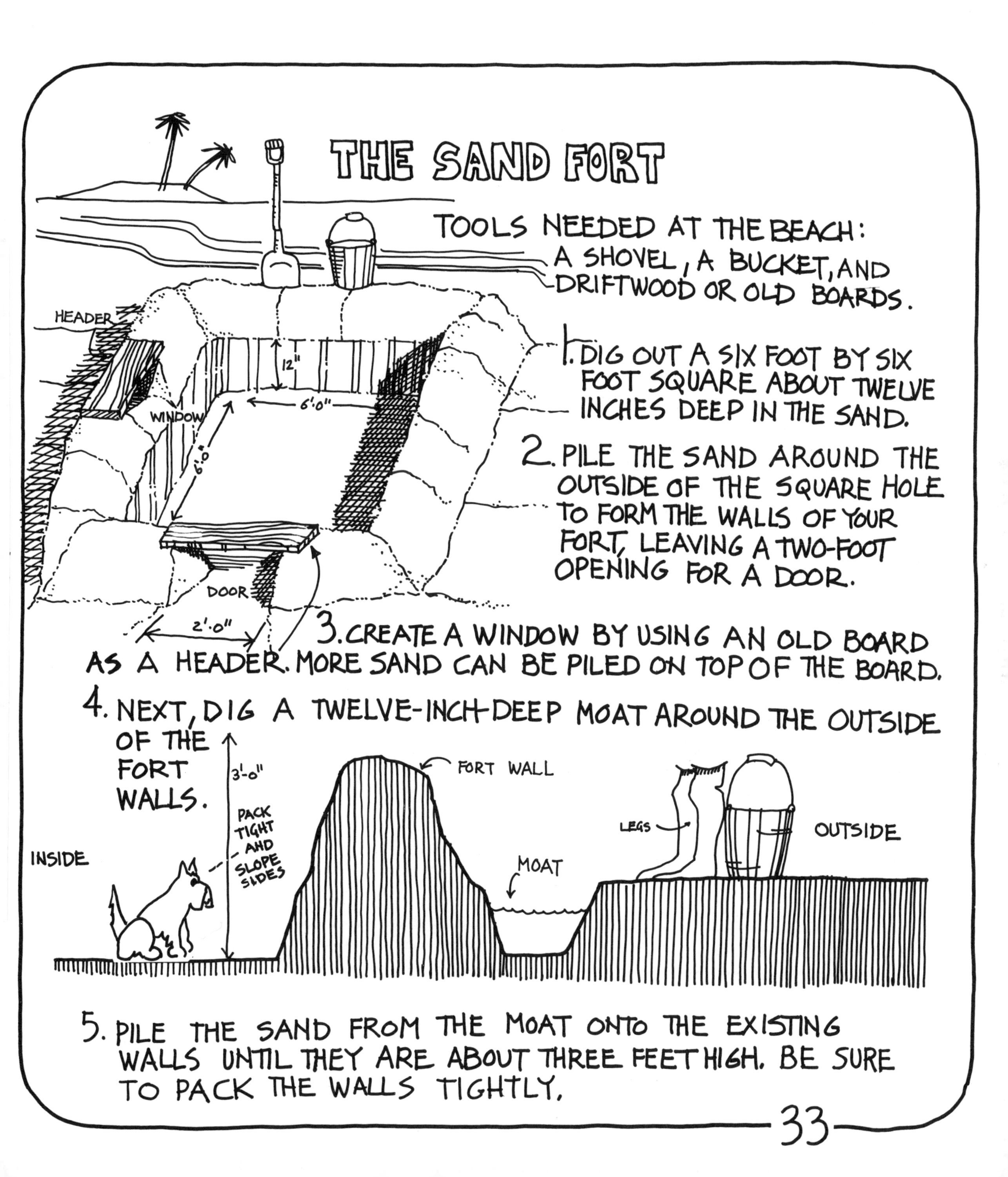
THE SAND FORT
TOOLS NEEDED AT THE BEACH:
A SHOVEL, A BUCKET, AND
DRIFTWOOD OR OLD BOARDS.
HEADER
12"
6'0"
WINDOW
6'0"
DOOR
2'0"
1. DIG OUT A SIX FOOT BY SIX
FOOT SQUARE ABOUT TWELVE
INCHES DEEP IN THE SAND.
2. PILE THE SAND AROUND THE
OUTSIDE OF THE SQUARE HOLE
TO FORM THE WALLS OF YOUR
FORT, LEAVING A TWO-FOOT
OPENING FOR A DOOR.
3. CREATE A WINDOW BY USING AN OLD BOARD
AS A HEADER. MORE SAND CAN BE PILED ON TOP OF THE BOARD.
4. NEXT, DIG A TWELVE-INCH-DEEP MOAT AROUND THE OUTSIDE
OF THE
FORT
WALLS.
3'-0"
PACK
TIGHT
AND
SLOPE
SIDES
FORT WALL
INSIDE
MOAT
LEGS
OUTSIDE
5. PILE THE SAND FROM THE MOAT ONTO THE EXISTING
WALLS UNTIL THEY ARE ABOUT THREE FEET HIGH. BE SURE
TO PACK THE WALLS TIGHTLY.
33

6. LAY STRONG BOARDS OR DRIFTWOOD ACROSS THE TOP OF THE WALLS AS A ROOF COVER. FOR ADDITIONAL SHADE DRAPE WITH BEACH TOWELS.

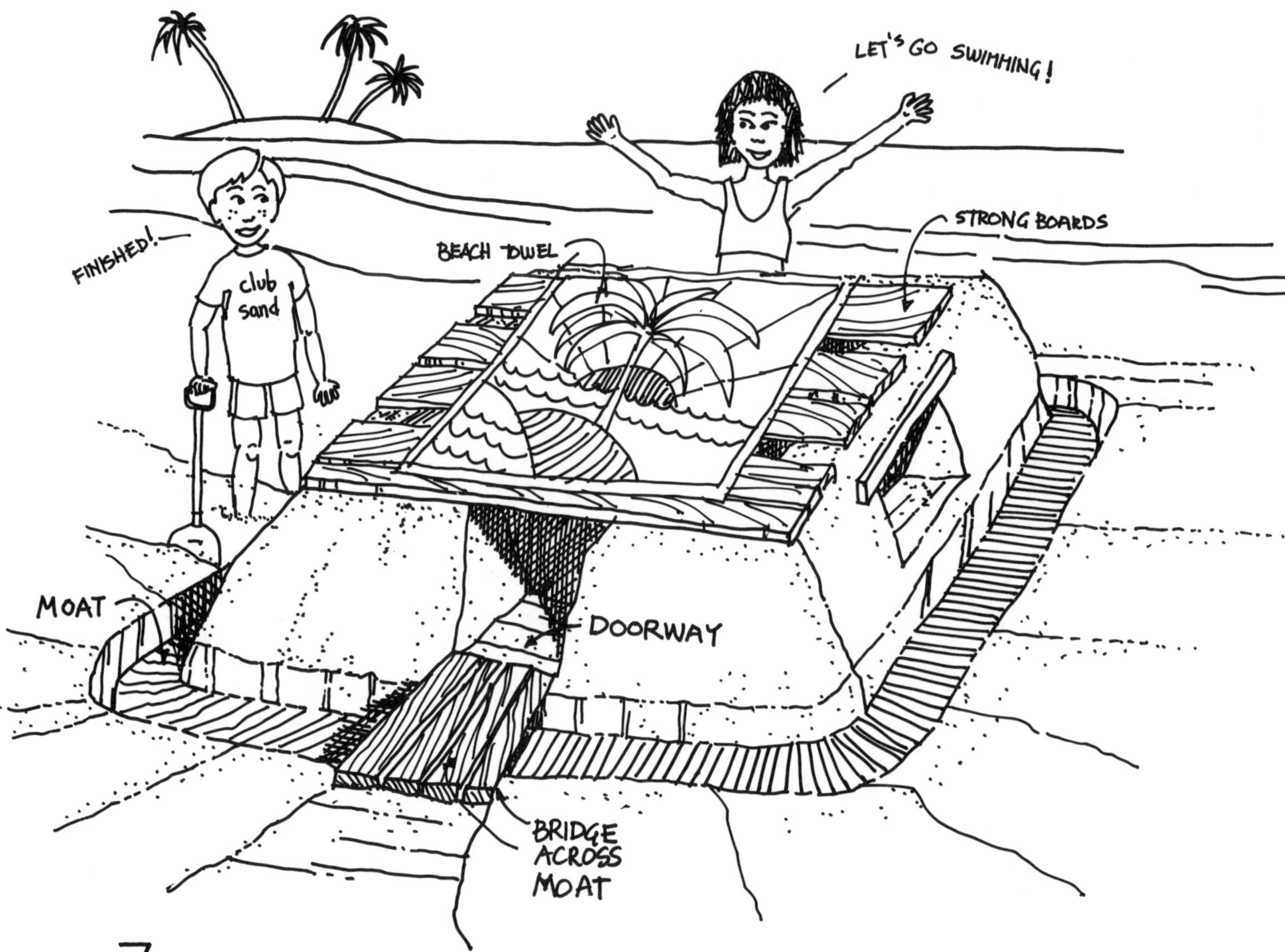

7. LEAN DRIFTWOOD OR BOARDS AT AN ANGLE AGAINST THE FORT MAKING A DOOR. THESE BOARDS CAN ALSO BE LAID DOWN TO MAKE A BRIDGE OVER THE MOAT.

SNOW
FORTS

IF YOU ARE LUCKY ENOUGH TO LIVE WHERE YOU HAVE SNOW IN THE WINTER, TRY ONE OF THESE FORTS. A COUPLE OF INCHES OF THE FLUFFY STUFF IS ALL YOU REALLY NEED — THAT, AND A GOOD PAIR OF MITTENS.

THE SNOWBALL FORT

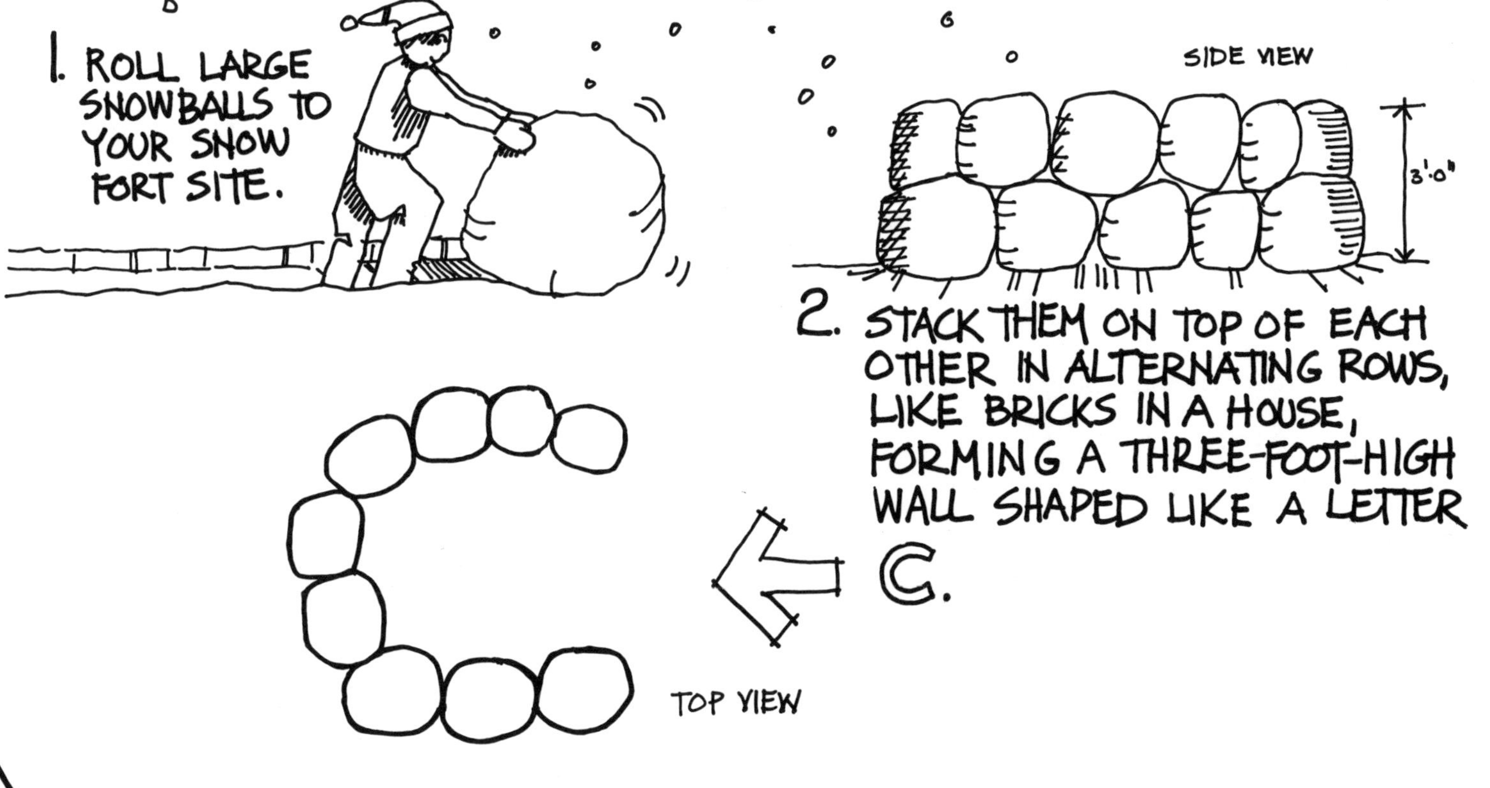

3. PUT WINDOWS IN THE WALL USING PIECES OF WOOD AS HEADERS.

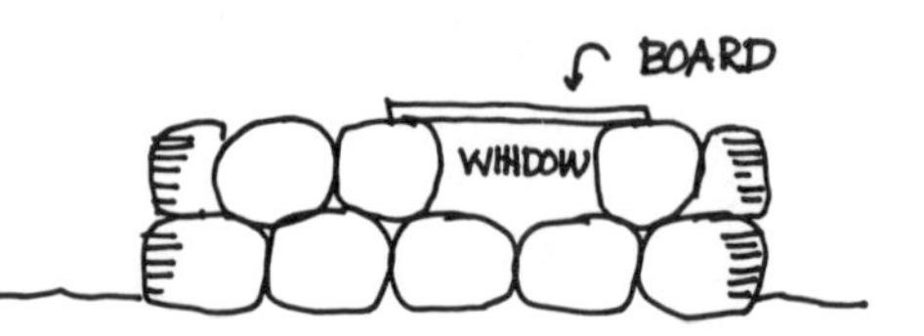

4. BUILD A TALLER WALL ACROSS THE TOP ONE-THIRD OF THE C LEAVING A TWO-FOOT OPENING FOR A DOORWAY.

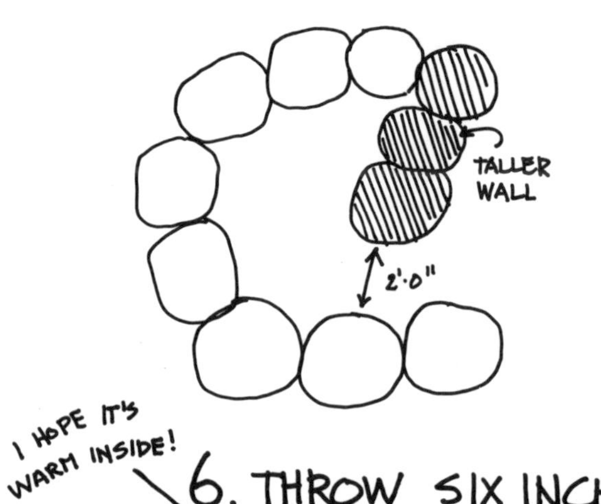

5. LAY BOARDS FROM THIS TALLER WALL SLANTING DOWN TO THE THREE-FOOT WALL.

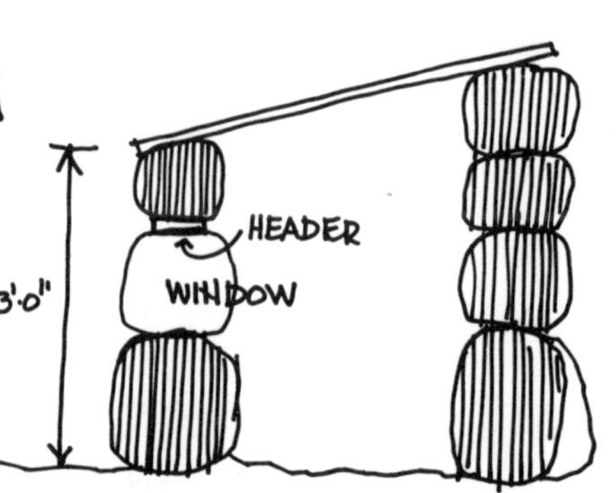

6. THROW SIX INCHES OF LOOSE SNOW ON TOP OF THE BOARDS TO HELP HOLD THEM IN PLACE.

AS A GREAT "WARM-UP" FOR YOUR NEW CREATION, TRY A FAMILY TREK OUT TO YOUR SNOW FORT AT NIGHT.

SIT ON FOAM PADS, MUNCH A SNACK, AND ENJOY.

THE SNOW TRENCH FORT

1. FIND A LARGE PILE OF SNOW, OR PILE WHAT SNOW YOU HAVE ON THE GROUND INTO A MOUND AT LEAST THREE FEET HIGH. (OF COURSE IF YOU ARE LUCKY ENOUGH TO HAVE THREE FEET OF SNOW EVERYWHERE YOU LOOK YOU CAN BUILD YOUR FORT ANYWHERE YOU LIKE.)

2. DIG A TRENCH DEEP ENOUGH TO CRAWL IN BUT NOT MORE THAN THREE FEET WIDE.

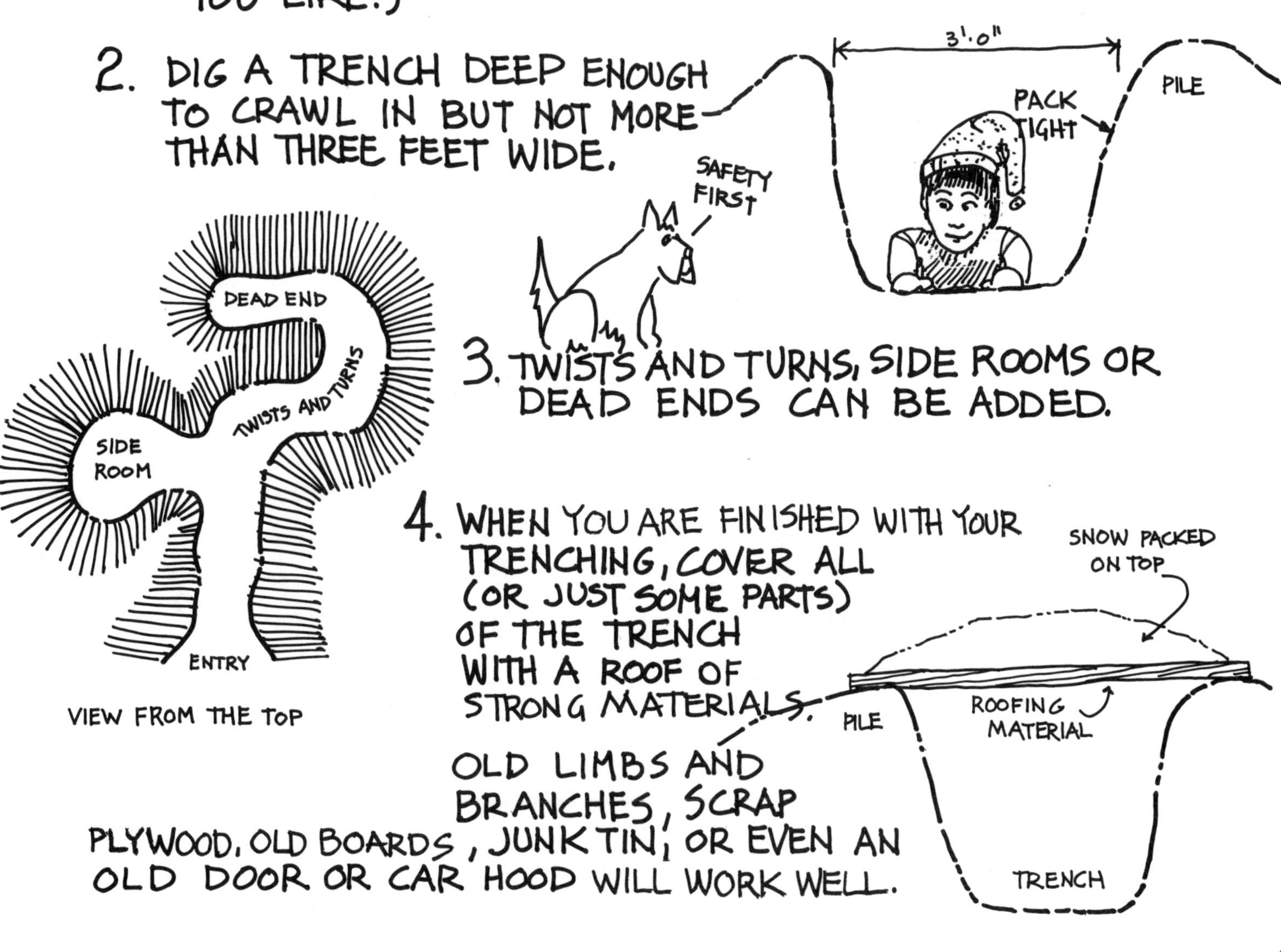

3. TWISTS AND TURNS, SIDE ROOMS OR DEAD ENDS CAN BE ADDED.

4. WHEN YOU ARE FINISHED WITH YOUR TRENCHING, COVER ALL (OR JUST SOME PARTS) OF THE TRENCH WITH A ROOF OF STRONG MATERIALS.

OLD LIMBS AND BRANCHES, SCRAP PLYWOOD, OLD BOARDS, JUNK TIN, OR EVEN AN OLD DOOR OR CAR HOOD WILL WORK WELL.

5. ANCHOR THE ROOF DOWN BY PACKING SNOW ON TOP.
6. MAKE A DOOR TO COVER THE TRENCH ENTRANCE USING AN OLD WOOL BLANKET OR PIECE OF PLYWOOD, AND YOU'RE ALL SET FOR COME WHAT MAY.
WHERE ARE THE KIDS?
MUST BE LUNCH TIME
TRENCH
COVERED ENTRY
SNOW PILE
PLYWOOD DOOR

THE IGLOO FORT

STRONG, WIND RESISTANT, AND AMAZINGLY SOUNDPROOF, THE IGLOO HAS SERVED THE ESKIMOS OF THE CANADIAN AND ALASKAN ARCTIC FOR CENTURIES.

BUILDING AN IGLOO IS NOT AN EASY TASK. IT TAKES TIME AND PATIENCE, PLUS SOME HELP FROM FRIENDS AND FAMILY (WHICH OF COURSE MAKES IT ALL THE MORE FUN TO BUILD).

1. BEGIN BY CUTTING LARGE BLOCKS OUT OF PACKED SNOW. A COOKIE SHEET OR A SAW WORKS VERY WELL AS A CUTTING TOOL.

2. USE THE EDGE TO SLICE DOWN INTO THE SNOW, CUTTING LOOSE ALL SIX SIDES OF A RECTANGULAR BLOCK, LIKE A SHOE BOX.

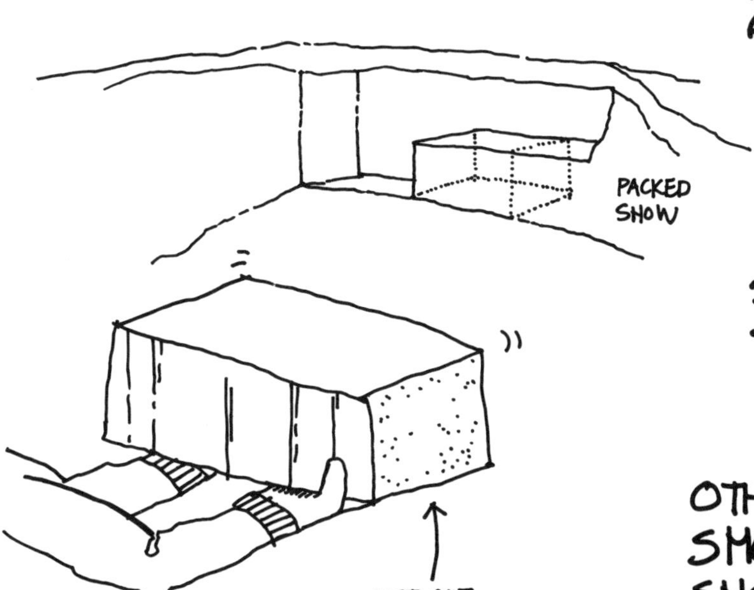

3. LIFT IT OUT WITH THE COOKIE SHEET OR YOUR HANDS. YOU NOW HAVE A SHAPE THAT WILL FIT NICELY TOGETHER WITH OTHER BLOCKS. THIS FORMS A VERY SMOOTH WALL—A SIGN OF TRUE SNOW CRAFTMANSHIP.

OR- IF YOU CAN'T CUT BLOCKS, BORROW A BREAD LOAF PAN FROM YOUR MOM OR DAD. PACK IT WITH SNOW AND THEN DUMP IT OUT. PRESTO- YOU'VE GOT SNOW BLOCKS.

4. START YOUR IGLOO WALL BY BUILDING A CIRCLE AS THE BASE OF YOUR FORT. DO NOT LEAVE A SPACE FOR A DOOR. YOU WILL CUT THAT OUT LATER.

AS YOU WORK AROUND THAT FIRST ROW OF BLOCKS, SLOPE THE TOP SLIGHTLY IN TOWARD THE CENTER.

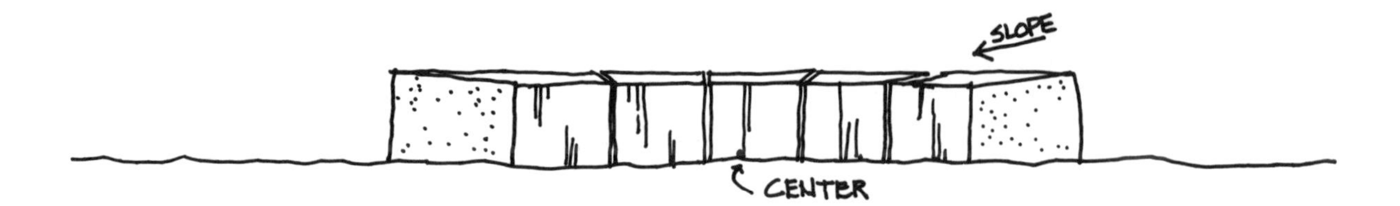

5. AFTER YOU HAVE COMPLETED THE BOTTOM ROW, CUT AWAY THE TOP OF THE BLOCKS INTO A SLOPING SPIRAL. IT SHOULD LOOK LIKE A ROAD GOING UP AND AROUND A MOUNTAIN.

START THE SECOND ROW OF BLOCKS. YOU WILL THEN BE BUILDING YOUR IGLOO IN AN UPWARD REACHING SPIRAL.

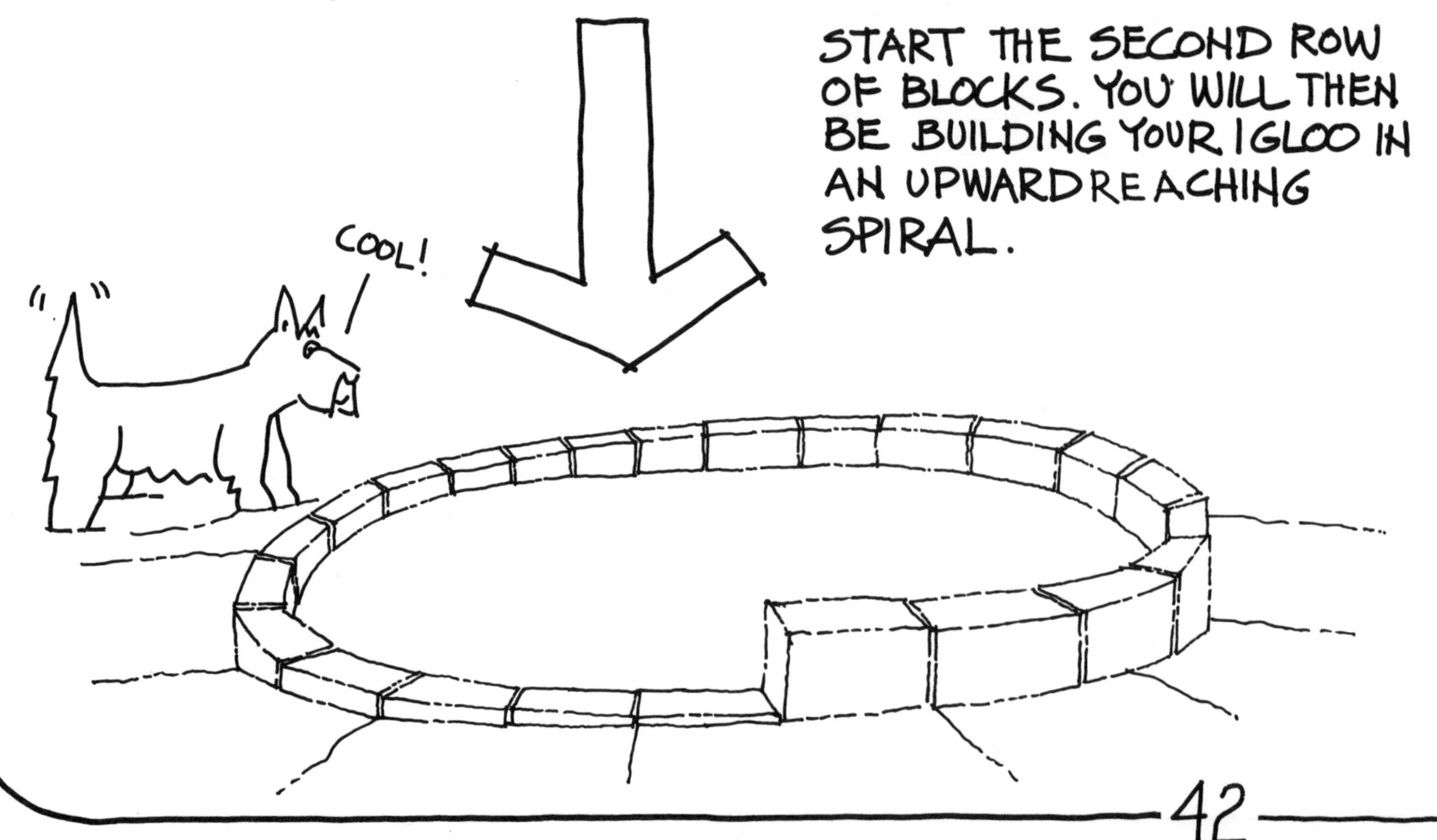

6. AS YOU BUILD EACH ROW OF BLOCKS YOU WILL WIND UP AND IN TOWARD THE CENTER, CREATING A DOME.
IT IS BEST TO KEEP THE WALLS CURVING IN TOWARD THE TOP EVENLY. THIS WILL HELP AVOID PROBLEMS WHEN PUTTING IN THE LAST FEW BLOCKS. TAKE YOUR TIME. WORK CAREFULLY.
7. AS YOU MAY HAVE IMAGINED, THE LAST FEW BLOCKS WILL LIE ALMOST PARALLEL TO THE FLOOR OF YOUR IGLOO. GRAVITY WILL PUT LOTS OF PRESSURE ON THESE BLOCKS TO FALL IN. HOWEVER, IF THE LOWER BLOCKS ARE FIRMLY PACKED IN PLACE, AND IF THE SPIRAL UP FROM THE BOTTOM IS EVEN, THE LAST BLOCKS WILL ALSO JAM FIRMLY INTO PLACE.
WATCH YOUR HEAD

8. AS SOON AS YOU HAVE FINISHED THE WALLS, TUNNEL DOWN UNDER THEM TO CREATE A TRENCH FOR A DOOR.

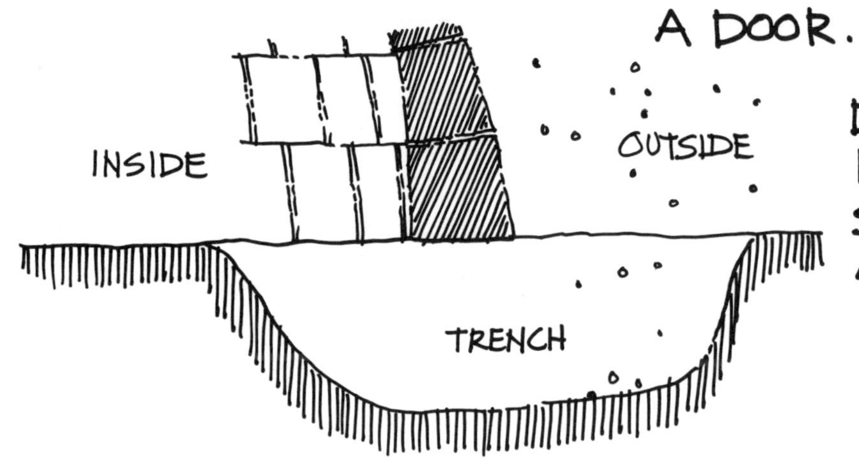

IF THE SNOW IS NOT DEEP ENOUGH, YOU MAY HAVE TO CUT THROUGH SOME OF THE WALL ALSO.

9. FILL IN THE CRACKS BETWEEN THE BLOCKS BY PRESSING AND PATTING SNOW INTO THEM.

10. **STOP** AT THIS POINT AND GIVE YOURSELF A PAT ON THE BACK...

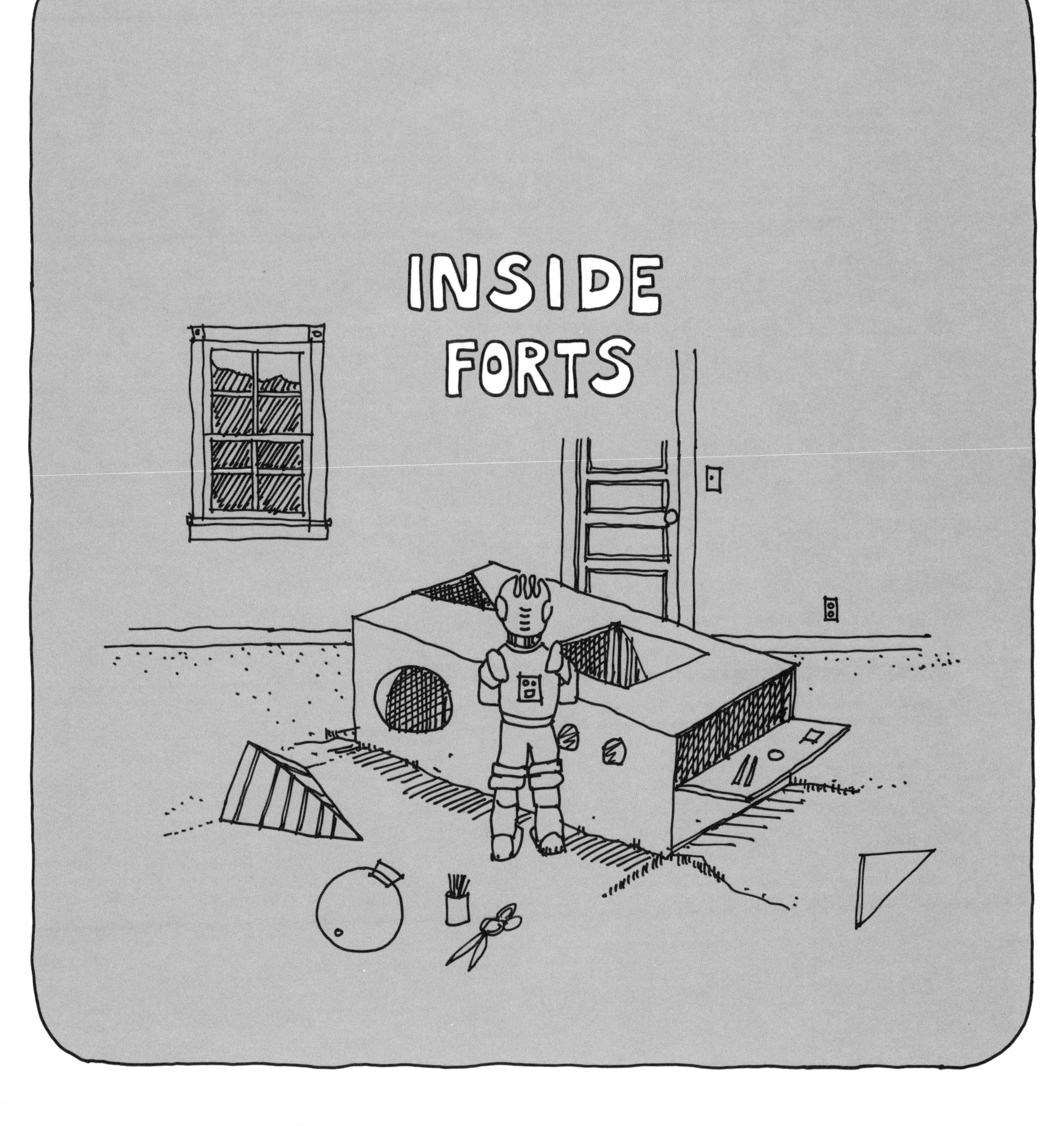
INSIDE
FORTS

CASTLES WITHIN YOUR CASTLE.

THERE ARE TIMES, SAD TO SAY, WHEN BUILDING A FORT OUTSIDE IS JUST NOT POSSIBLE. MAYBE YOU HAVE A COLD, OR IT'S RAINING CATS AND DOGS, OR YOU HAVE ONLY A FEW MINUTES TO SPARE.

DON'T GIVE UP. THERE'S ALWAYS THE **INSIDE FORT.**

FOLLOWING ARE SOME IDEAS FOR FORTS THAT USE COMMON HOUSEHOLD ITEMS, ARE SPEEDY TO SET UP, AND HAVE AN ALMOST INSTANT TEAR-DOWN TIME WHEN DINNER IS READY.

THE TABLE FORT

1. SINCE IT ALREADY HAS A ROOF, ALL YOU REALLY NEED ARE WALLS. THESE CAN BE ADDED EASILY BY USING BLANKETS DRAPED OVER THE TABLE AND TOUCHING THE FLOOR.

2. USE BOOKS OR MAGAZINES TO KEEP THE BLANKET FROM FALLING TO THE FLOOR. (NO NAILS OR THUMB TACKS PLEASE!)

THE SPLIT-LEVEL CHAIR FORT

1. TURN TWO CHAIRS BACK-TO-BACK LEAVING THREE FEET BETWEEN THEM.

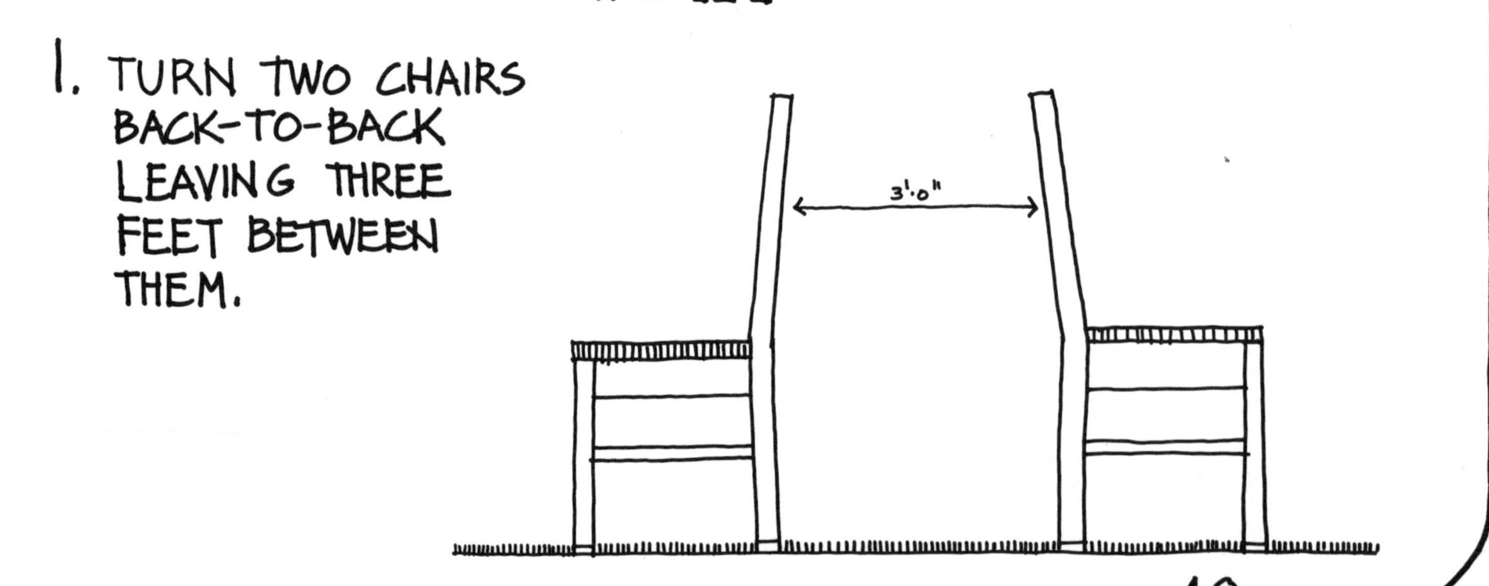

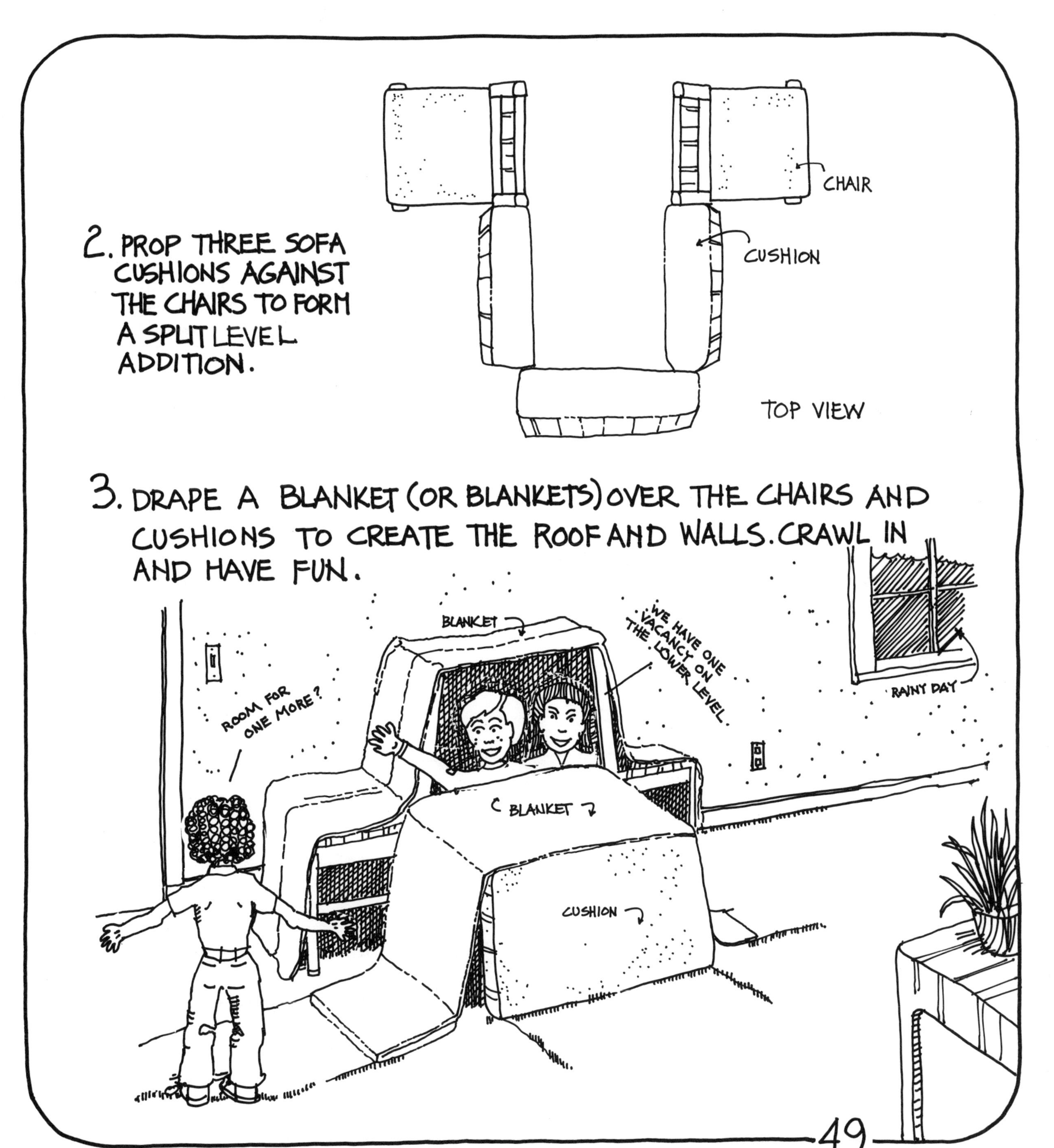
2. PROP THREE SOFA CUSHIONS AGAINST THE CHAIRS TO FORM A SPLIT LEVEL ADDITION.
CHAIR
CUSHION
TOP VIEW
3. DRAPE A BLANKET (OR BLANKETS) OVER THE CHAIRS AND CUSHIONS TO CREATE THE ROOF AND WALLS. CRAWL IN AND HAVE FUN.
BLANKET
WE HAVE ONE VACANCY ON THE LOWER LEVEL
RAINY DAY
ROOM FOR ONE MORE?
BLANKET
CUSHION

THE BE-TWIN FORT

1. BEGIN BY FINDING A BOX LARGE ENOUGH TO SPAN THE GAP BETWEEN TWO TWIN BEDS.

2. USING A KNIFE OR SCISSORS, CUT SOME OBSERVATION WINDOWS.

3. POSITION THE BOX AS SHOWN AND PLACE BLANKETS ACROSS THE REST OF THE OPENING, SECURING THEM WITH BOOKS.

4. FINALLY, LAY A BROOM ACROSS THE FOOT OF THE BEDS FOR A DOORWAY HEADER AND DRAPE TWO TOWELS OVER IT FOR DOUBLE DOORS, SECURING THEM WITH SAFETY PINS.

THE DESK FORT

1. FIRST, PUT THE DESK CHAIR OUT OF THE WAY. YOU WON'T NEED IT.

2. USING SOFA OR LOUNGE CHAIR CUSHIONS, LEAN THEM AGAINST EACH OTHER, CREATING A TUNNEL LEADING INTO THE VACANT DESK CHAIR SPACE.

3. DRAPE A BLANKET OR TOWEL OVER THE CUSHIONS TO COVER THE CRACKS.

4. FINALLY, ANCHOR A BLANKET TO THE DESKTOP WITH BOOKS AND HANG IT OVER THE EDGE, SEALING OFF THE GAP BETWEEN THE CUSHIONS AND THE DESK CHAIR SPACE.

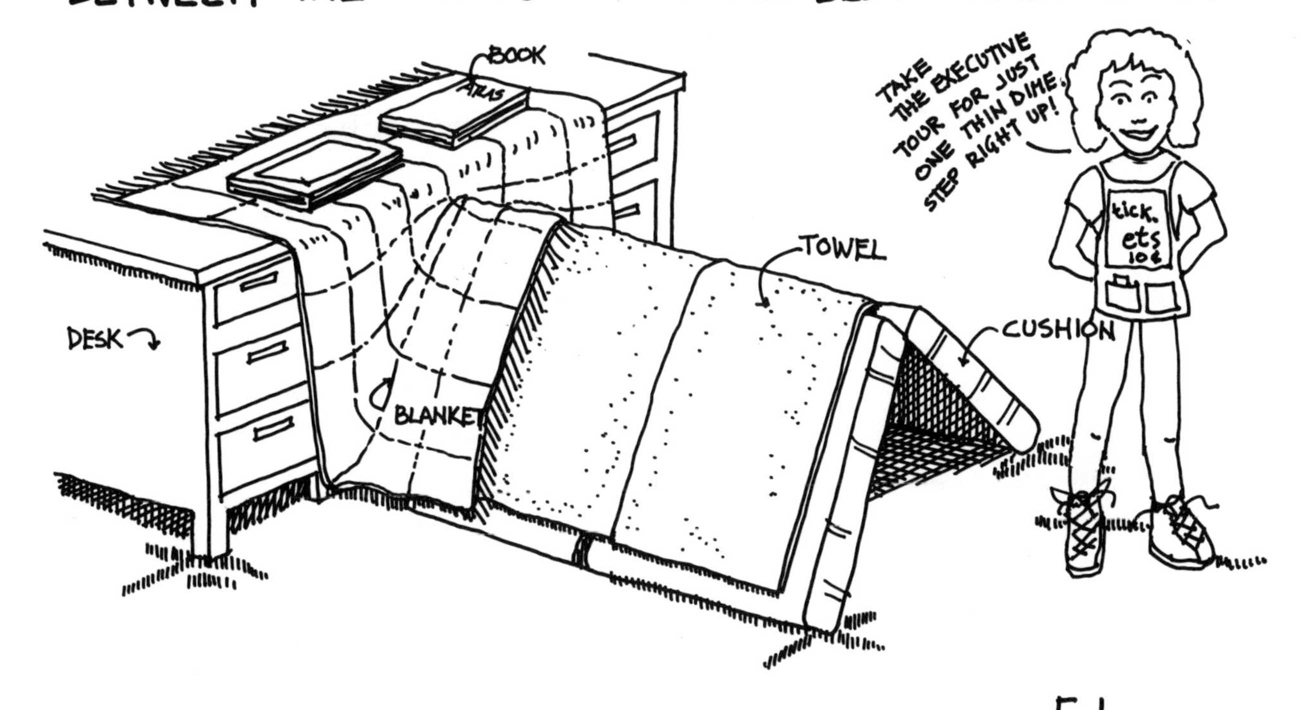

THE SPACE BOX FORT

THE SPACE BOX FORT TAKES LONGER TO BUILD THAN OTHER INSIDE FORTS, AND REQUIRES SPECIAL MATERIALS AND TOOLS.

BUT WHEN FINISHED, IT IS A VEHICLE FOR OUTER SPACE EXPLORATION PARKED AND WAITING RIGHT INSIDE YOUR OWN HOME. A GREAT CHALLENGE FOR CREATIVE FORT BUILDERS, IT CAN TRAVEL AS FAST AND AS FAR AS YOUR IMAGINATION WILL ALLOW.

TO BUILD ONE YOU WILL NEED:

- ☐ A REFRIGERATOR BOX (CHECK FOR ONE AT A LOCAL APPLIANCE STORE)
- ☐ A MEDIUM-SIZED CARDBOARD BOX
- ☐ A UTILITY KNIFE OR A BREAD KNIFE
- ☐ STRING
- ☐ A ROLL OF STRONG TAPE (2" DUCT TAPE WORKS WELL)

EASY! THEY ARE SHARP. ASK AN ADULT TO HELP.

1. TO START, LAY THE BOX ON ITS SIDE AND CUT A CIRCULAR-SHAPED DOOR NEAR THE BACK OF THE SPACESHIP. (TRACE AROUND A GARBAGE CAN LID.) SAVE THE ROUND PIECE OF CARDBOARD.

2. BEGIN THE CONSTRUCTION OF THE ASTRONAUT'S FRONT OBSERVATION WINDOW BY CUTTING ACROSS THE TOP OF THE SPACESHIP'S NOSE AND DOWN THE SIDES.

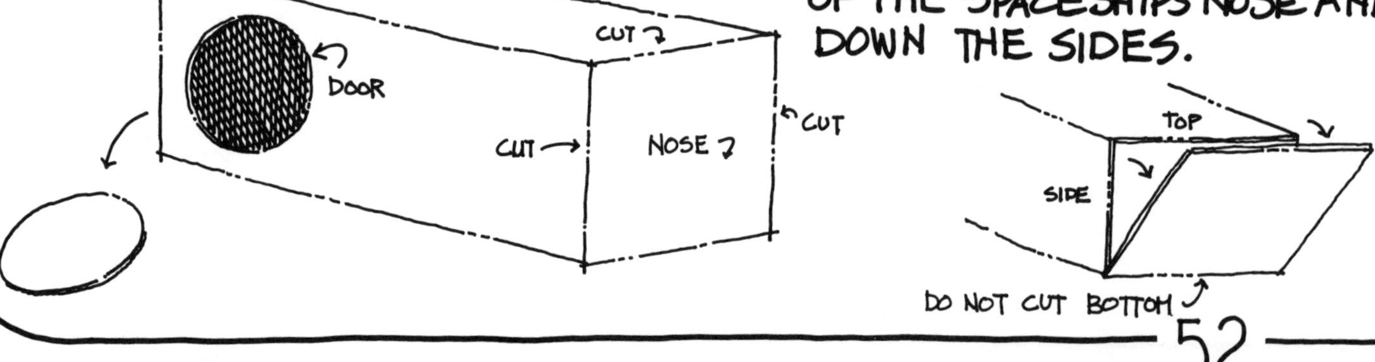

3. FROM THE OUTSIDE, MARK A LINE HALF-WAY DOWN THE NOSE.

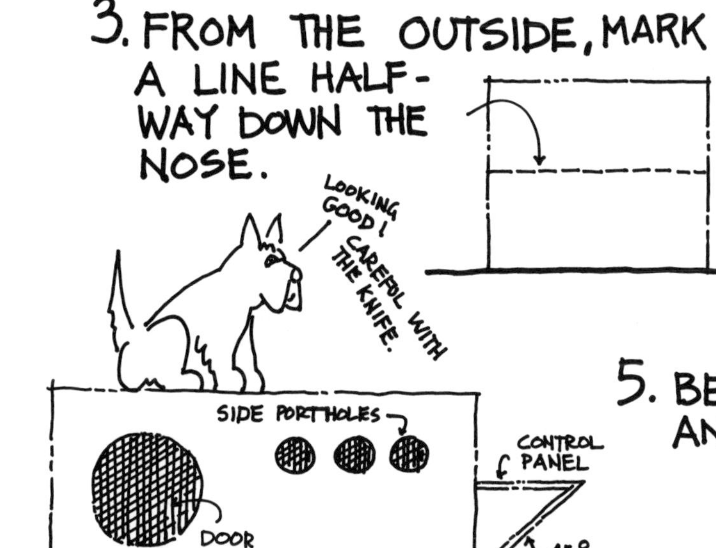

4. SCORE THIS LINE WITH YOUR KNIFE. (THAT MEANS CUT ALONG THE LINE HALFWAY THROUGH THE CARDBOARD.

KNIFE
CARDBOARD
½ THICKNESS

5. BEND THE BOTTOM HALF OUT AT A 45° ANGLE AND FOLD THE TOP HALF DOWN UNTIL IT IS PARALLEL TO THE FLOOR. THIS FLAT SURFACE WILL BE YOUR CONTROL PANEL. TAPE IT IN PLACE.

6. CUT SIDE PORTHOLES ON EACH SIDE OF THE BOX. SAUCERS OR SMALL PLATES WORK WELL FOR TRACING.

7. NEXT, LAY THE MEDIUM-SIZED CARDBOARD BOX ON TOP OF THE SPACESHIP. TRACE AROUND IT TO MARK LINES FOR CUTTING THE STELLAR LOOKOUT BAY. CUT OUT THE MARKED RECTANGLE.

STELLAR LOOKOUT BAY
WINDOW
CUT OUT

8. CUT WINDOWS IN THE BOX SIDES, AND REMOVE THE BOX FLAPS. PLACE THE BOX UPSIDE DOWN OVER THE LOOKOUT BAY HOLE AND TAPE IT SECURELY DOWN.

9. TO CREATE A TAIL FIN, TAKE THE BOX TOP YOU JUST CUT OFF AND CUT IT INTO A TRIANGLE. SCORE A LINE DOWN THE MIDDLE OF THE TRIANGLE. FOLD ALONG THIS LINE AND TAPE THE FIN TO THE REAR OF THE SPACESHIP.

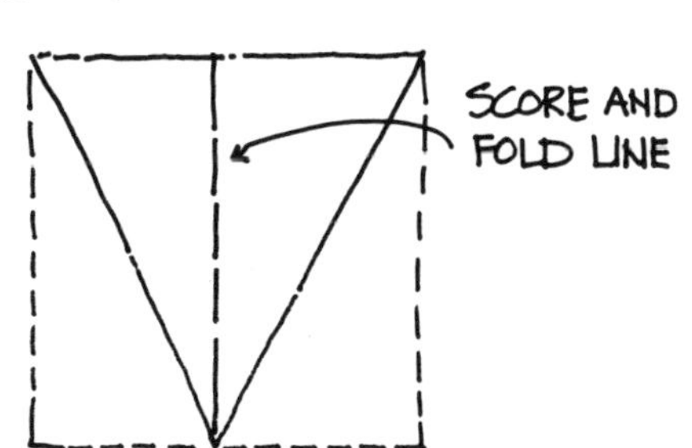

10. LAST, TAPE THE AIR-LOCK DOOR ONTO THE SPACESHIP, CREATING A HINGE ON ONE SIDE.
JUMP IN, BLAST OFF, AND ENJOY THE RIDE!
TAIL FIN
LOOK OUT BAY
PREPARE FOR BLAST OFF!
CAPTAIN
CHECK WITH CAPTAIN BEFORE OPENING
AIR LOCK DOOR
HINGE
CONTROL PANEL
KELSEY'S SPACE ROCKET
REPORTING AS ORDERED, CAPTAIN.
crew
I GET TO RIDE IN THE TAIL FIN!
Space dog
Space bone

THE FINISHING TOUCHES

THE INSIDE OF YOUR FORT

FIXING UP THE INSIDE OF A FORT IS A VERY PERSONAL THING (EVEN WHEN DONE BY A LARGE GROUP). LIKE YOUR ROOM AT HOME, YOUR FORT SHOULD BE COMFORTABLE, USEFUL, AND AT THE SAME TIME A PART OF WHAT YOU ARE AS A PERSON.

FOR SOME FORT BUILDERS THIS MEANS THE INSIDES OF THEIR FORTS ARE CLUTTERED WITH ALL SORTS OF THINGS—FROM MOSS ON THE FLOOR TO PICTURES ON THE WALLS. FOR OTHERS, THIS MEANS THAT THEY DON'T FIX UP THE INSIDES OF THEIR FORTS AT ALL. THEY JUST ENJOY IT AS IT IS. AND THERE ARE MANY PEOPLE IN-BETWEEN WHO NEITHER CLUTTER THEIR FORT NOR LEAVE IT BARE.

IF YOU ARE ONE OF THOSE WHO WANT TO FIX UP THE INSIDE OF YOUR FORT, OR AT LEAST ARE INTERESTED IN HOW OTHERS DO IT, HERE ARE SOME SUGGESTIONS FOR OUTSIDE FORTS (INCLUDING SNOW FORTS) THAT YOU MIGHT FIND HELPFUL*:

- COVER THE GROUND WITH MOSS, PINE NEEDLES, OR HAY. THIS MAKES A SOFT, DRY FLOOR.
- FIND SCRAP PLYWOOD OR BOARDS AND COVER THE FLOOR. THIS WOOD CAN EVEN BE COVERED WITH OLD CARPET OR RUGS. FOR SECRET STORAGE OF VALUABLE ITEMS, DIG A HOLE IN THE FLOOR AND PLACE A BOARD OVER IT.

* COURTESY OF FIFTH-GRADE STUDENTS, OCEANLAKE SCHOOL, LINCOLN CITY, OREGON

- COVER THE WALLS WITH OLD RUGS OR CARPET. THIS HELPS KEEP YOUR FORT WARMER AND QUIETER AND IS PLEASING TO LOOK AT.
- HANG THINGS ON THE WALLS: PICTURES, RACKS TO HOLD BELONGINGS, AN OLD MEDICINE CABINET, OR EVEN A MIRROR.
- BUILD LITTLE CAVES IN THE WALLS FOR STORAGE OR TO DISPLAY VALUABLE ITEMS. FOR SECRET STORAGE, THESE MINIATURE CAVES CAN BE CONCEALED BY HANGING SOMETHING IN FRONT OF THEM.
- ADD FURNITURE TO YOUR FORT. WOODEN CRATES, BOXES, OR OLD TIRES MAKE GOOD CHAIRS. LARGE PIECES OF FIREWOOD SET ON END CAN BE USED IN THE SAME WAY. OLD DISCARDED FURNITURE CAN BE RIGGED UP TO BE USEFUL . . . CHAIRS, CARD TABLES, EVEN BOOK CASES.
- DECORATE WITH POTTERY, FLOWERS, SCRAP MATERIALS, ORIGINAL DRAWINGS AND ART WORK, COLLECTED STONES, SHELLS, LEAVES, ETC.
- BE CREATIVE.

FOR INSIDE FORTS, TRY THESE IDEAS:

- ☐ LINE YOUR FORT WITH PILLOWS, INCLUDING THE FLOOR.
- ☐ USE A STRING TO HANG A FLASHLIGHT FROM THE CEILING.
- ☐ PUT A SMALL LAMP IN YOUR FORT. (CAUTION: DON'T COVER THE TOP OF THE LAMPSHADE WITH ANYTHING. IT CAN START A FIRE!)
- ☐ FASTEN YOUR FAVORITE POSTER TO THE WALL.
- ☐ USE A BOX TO MAKE A SEPARATE STORAGE COMPARTMENT FOR YOUR FAVORITE THINGS.
- ☐ IF IT'S O K WITH YOUR MOM AND DAD, PUT THE TV IN YOUR FORT TO WATCH YOUR FAVORITE SHOW.
- ☐ MAKE COLORED PAPER STREAMERS TO HANG IN YOUR FORT.
- ☐ CUT OUT TWENTY PICTURES OF EYES FROM AN OLD MAGAZINE AND TAPE THEM UP FOR A FORT CONVENTION.
- ☐ MAKE BEDS FOR YOUR STUFFED ANIMALS.
- ☐ BUILD A TUNNEL INTO YOUR FORT FOR CARS OR TRUCKS.
- ☐ USE A BOX AND PILLOWCASE TO MAKE A SMALL TABLE. INVITE SOME FRIENDS OR FAMILY IN FOR A SNACK.
- ☐ CARPET YOUR FORT WITH TOWELS.
- ☐ STICK YOUR FAVORITE BOOKS OR COMICS IN YOUR FORT FOR A GOOD READING NOOK.
- ☐ DRAW OR CUT OUT PICTURES OF ANIMALS AND DECORATE THE WALLS.

RULES
1. HAVE
2. FUN
HIGH-LAND KIDS CLUB
PICKLES
Shade for rent
WOOF

THE GRAND FINALE

PUTTING THE FINISHING TOUCHES ON ANY KIND OF FORT CAN GO ON FOR ITS ENTIRE LIFE: A NEW ENTRANCE HERE, AN EXTRA LAYER OF LEAVES THERE, A PICTURE, A SHELF, A CARD TABLE. THIS IS VERY NORMAL. BUT... EVEN WITH ALL OF THIS EXTRA ATTENTION TO DETAIL, THERE COMES A TIME WHEN IN YOUR MIND YOU THINK, "MY FORT IS FINISHED!" AT THIS POINT YOU HAVE COME UPON AN OCCASION FOR CELEBRATION AND CEREMONY. NOW IS THE TIME TO MAKE IT OFFICIAL.

IF YOUR FORT IS THE PRIVATE KIND, KNOWN ONLY TO CLUB MEMBERS, YOU WILL PROBABLY WANT TO HAVE A SECRET CEREMONY. THERE IS SOMETHING ESPECIALLY DELICIOUS ABOUT DOING IT THIS WAY. SNEAKING OFF WITH THAT SMALL GROUP OF FRIENDS (OR MAYBE EVEN JUST YOURSELF) IS GREAT FUN. YOU MAY HAVE A HIDDEN TRAIL TO YOUR FORT OR A SECRET DOOR.

OFTEN ENTRANCE TO SUCH A FORT IS GAINED ONLY BY KNOWING A SECRET PASSWORD. THIS CAN RANGE FROM SOMETHING SIMPLE LIKE "SWORDFISH" TO LONGER SENTENCES, SUCH AS "THE WARRIOR DANCES BY THE FULL MOON." SERIES OF NUMBERS AND LETTERS (Z23J940Q), NONSENSE WORDS ("ALLIGASO" OR "NUMZUCKLE"), SECRET HANDSHAKES, AND SECRET KNOCKS ALSO WORK WELL.

ONCE GATHERED IN YOUR FORT, YOU CAN TALK ABOUT THE FORT, HOW IT WAS BUILT, WHO HELPED, AND HOW IT IS TO BE USED. CLOSELY HELD SECRETS MAY BE SPOKEN THERE, NEVER TO BE REPEATED IN ANY OTHER PLACE. YOU HAVE GIVEN YOUR FORT A SPECIAL MAGIC, A PRIVACY SHARED BY ONLY A FEW.

THIS IS AN IMPORTANT POINT, AND FOR SOME PEOPLE IT IS THE BEST USE OF A FORT. THERE IS SOMETHING VERY SPECIAL ABOUT SITTING DOWN IN YOUR OWN HANDMADE SHELTER AND SHARING SECRETS THAT MAKES PEOPLE FEEL REALLY GOOD ABOUT EACH OTHER. YOU'VE SHOWN SOMEONE SOMETHING ABOUT YOURSELF YOU DIDN'T THINK YOU EVER WOULD, OR COULD.

THE PROBLEM THAT COMES UP MOST WHEN A FORT IS USED AS A PRIVATE CLUBHOUSE IS WHO CAN USE IT. BECAUSE CERTAIN PEOPLE BUILT IT, THEY SOMETIMES FEEL THEY WANT TO EXCLUDE OR STOP ALL OTHERS FROM COMING AROUND. THIS IS A PART OF HUMAN NATURE. WE ALL WANT TO PROTECT WHAT IS OURS.

SO... WE GET TORN BETWEEN WANTING TO KEEP OUT THAT NEW KID FROM SCHOOL OR FROM DOWN THE STREET AND REMEMBERING WHAT IT FELT LIKE WHEN WE WERE LEFT OUT OF SOMETHING REALLY NEAT. IT'S NOT EASY FOR ANYONE INVOLVED.

PUTTING YOURSELF IN ANOTHER KID'S PLACE HELPS YOU SEE THAT PERSON'S POINT OF VIEW AND UNDERSTAND WHAT THAT PERSON MIGHT BE FEELING. REMEMBERING THAT FORTS ARE FOR FUN CAN BE A BIG HELP IN DECIDING WHAT TO DO.

ON THE OTHER HAND, YOUR FORT MAY BE A VERY OPEN, PUBLIC PLACE. IT MAY BE THE KIND THAT WAS BUILT WITH LOTS OF HELP FROM LOTS OF PEOPLE — MOM, DAD, BROTHERS AND SISTERS, FRIENDS FROM DOWN THE STREET AND ACROSS THE COUNTRY, THE NEIGHBORS, DISTANT RELATIVES, AND EVEN THE U.P.S. DRIVER AND THE MAIL CARRIER.

IF THIS IS THE CASE, A LESS SECRET CELEBRATION IS CALLED FOR. ADULTS CALL IT AN "OPEN HOUSE". YOU MIGHT LABEL IT A "FANTASTIC FORT FAIR."

INVITE EVERYONE TO SEE YOUR FORT. GIVE TOURS. EXPLAIN HOW THE FORT WAS BUILT, WHO HELPED, AND HOW IT WILL BE USED. PRESENT CERTIFICATES OF APPRECIATION TO THOSE WHO HELPED. SING SONGS. HAVE A HOT DOG ROAST. CUT A RIBBON FROM ACROSS THE MAIN ENTRANCE AND PILE EVERYONE INSIDE.

I DECLARE-
THIS FORT
OPEN!
CER
OF
APPREC-
IATION
TOURS
WHERE'S THE
HOT DOGS?
YOU'VE GOT IT NOW! SOMETHING
SPECIAL. YOUR VERY OWN HANDMADE
FORT.